HOME FREE

A HIGHER ELEVATIONS NOVEL

JODI PAYNE

BA TORTUGA

Home Free

Cover illustration by AJ Corza
http://www.seeingstatic.com/
Cover content is for illustrative purposes only and any person depicted on the cover is a model.

ISBN: 978-1-951011-89-5

Published by Tygerseye Publishing, LLC
July 2023
Printed in the USA

HOME FREE

Jodi Payne & BA Tortuga

Connor Westin and Early Jericho have a comfortable, busy life in Denver. Connor is a lawyer who brings home the bacon and Early is a stay at home dad to their two young boys.

Sure, Early is a cowboy at heart, but he loves their kids and as far as Connor is concerned they're happy in their suburban home.

When Early inherits a ranch on the Western Slope of Colorado, neither is sure what they should do about it. That is until they visit, and Connor sees just how much it all means to his husband.

Both men agree to uproot their family and take a shot at running the ranch together, but it takes time to shut down one life and start another. Early takes the boys to the ranch while Connor spends the summer in Denver to handle all the details of moving on.

Between the long distance, the new responsibilities, and interference from a not so well meaning employee, Connor and Early have trouble staying connected. Will the ranch become the home they need it to be, or will it tear their family apart?

THE HIGHER ELEVATION SERIES

All true standalone titles that can be read in any order.

Bigger Than Us

Keeping Promises

Home Free

Heart of a Cowboy

To our wives

1

Connor Westin parked his BMW in the garage and climbed out, his phone switching from Bluetooth to speaker automatically. "Agree to fixing the window and the lock on the back door, but the kitchen appliances are as-is, and we're not painting anything. That's ridiculous."

"You want me to say it's ridiculous?"

Connor reminded himself that although Kit was a great paralegal, he was young. "That would be fun, wouldn't it?"

"So, no. Got it." Kit was also way too serious.

"Thank you. I'm around if they come back with anything tonight. Gotta run." He hung up, dropped his phone in his pocket, and went into the house. "Smells good in here." He made his way to the kitchen, where he knew his handsome husband would be cooking dinner for their family.

"Chicken parm. Your sons had a request." Early wore a pair of jeans and a T-shirt, button-down shirt draped over one of the dining room chairs. Pretty-pretty. "How goes it?"

"Good, another day another house sale. And there's some easement dispute downtown that I'm supposed to be talking to someone about tomorrow." He slid a hand around

Early's waist, fingers spreading out across killer abs and kissed his nape. "*My* sons? What did they do now?"

"Which one?" Early shot him a quick, easy grin. "Jaxson climbed behind the bleachers and found a mouse, which he proceeded to keep in his lunch box until he got ready to come home, and he showed it to Jenny Franklin. It's now living in a cage in his room, his lunch box has been bleached, and I made him apologize to the teacher and Jenny. And Jayden..."

Oh god.

"He apparently climbed into the ceiling of the school using the pipes in the boys' bathroom. Did you know he's allergic to fiberglass? He is. He looks vaguely like he's been boiled. I'm calling him Lobster Boy. He isn't amused."

Oh, the poor kid. That had to itch. "Good. Great. They're both still alive and taking after you." Truth be told, Jayden was more like him in this case, but he wasn't going to admit it.

"Dad! I got a mouse. You wanna see?"

"Has it had its shots?"

"What?"

He glanced at Early. "We're keeping the mouse?"

"You going to poison it?" Early shrugged, altogether too unconcerned about a possible disease-ridden rodent in their house.

"Daddy! His name is Dennis. You can't kill it if it has a name."

Connor sighed. "I didn't mean we should kill it. Geez. But maybe Mrs. Mouse misses him?" It was worth a shot.

"He's not married. He's a DJ, and he's going to be all about the bass." Save him from smartass sons.

"DJ Dennis Mouse?" He ruffled Jaxson's hair. "Fine. But he's going to the vet."

"Okay! Wanna meet him?"

Early shook his head. "After supper. Y'all have fifteen minutes. Go wash and tell Lobster Boy to get his butt down here."

Jaxson bounced up and ran for the stairs. "Lostber Boy! Daddy says get your butt butt butt down here!"

"Stop calling me that!" Jayden came slumping down the stairs and shuffled into the kitchen. "Hi, Dad," he said opening the fridge door and hiding behind it.

"Hey, kid. So, what was the endgame here? After you made it into the ceiling?"

"Endgame?"

"What were you trying to do?"

Jayden closed the fridge door and looked at him, clearly confused. He was definitely red and swollen. "I don't know. I just did it."

"We're raising monkeys." Connor shook his head. "Set the table, boys."

Early just went about his business like nothing was out of the ordinary and, really, nothing was. This was par for the course. "So that was my day."

"Just another day in paradise. Did he get some Benadryl?"

"Benadryl, oatmeal bath, cortisone cream—he got the whole enchilada." Early rolled his eyes and started moving food to the table.

"You're a good dad." Connor gave Early one more quick hug, then hung up his coat so he could help. "What can I do?"

"Salad. Green beans. Something healthy that we have to force our children to eat."

"There's leftover broccoli." There was always leftover broccoli because their kids were not good eaters. He opened up the fridge, grabbed the bowl, and stuck in the microwave.

Early seemed...tired, maybe? Something felt a little dull, a little off. Not enough to worry about, he supposed. It was the end of another incredibly busy day with two active boys. He hoped the kids hadn't brought a bug home; it was so close to the end of the school year.

He grabbed the bowl and carried it carefully into the dining room, setting down right in front of Jaxson. "It's hot guys, careful."

"Yay. Limp trees."

Early's growl was immediate. "You watch it, or I'll serve nothing but brussels sprouts for a week."

Oh, god. Not that. Not again.

Never again.

He reached over and put two florets on each of the kids' plates. "No arguments." Then he took some for himself because he actually liked broccoli. "Chicken parm was a good call, though." He served them each some of that too, and himself before handing Early the plate. "Looks as good as it smells, honey."

"Thanks." Early chuckled and shook his head. "So, we've survived another school day. Go team Jericho."

"Oh they're yours again now, huh? Why? Because I didn't lose my mind over the mouse?" Connor grinned at Early, teasing.

"He's a nice mouse, Dad!"

He rolled his eyes. "Eat. Jayden, tell me about the math test."

Jayden gave him a deadpan look. "You mean the one that I aced?"

He laughed. "I guess that's the one. Nice work."

"I got done early, that's when I—"

"I don't really need the details unless the principal calls me."

Jayden arched one eyebrow, somehow looking just like Early. "Principal Shields always calls Daddy. She thinks he's hot. She calls him 'Mister Early' and puts her hand on his arm."

He mimicked that look, giving it to Early instead. "He is hot, but he's mine." And Principal Shields probably didn't want to talk to him anyway, he'd been deemed "less reasonable" a few years back.

"Dad! Ew! That's nasty!" Jaxson gagged dramatically, slumping against his brother, sending his fork flying, red sauce spraying across the floor.

"Jax! Ugh." He sighed and got up, going for a damp towel. And another fork. "I know we taught you table manners at some point. Daddy insists on it." He brought the towel back and handed it to Jaxson, then traded a clean fork for the one that landed on the floor. "Clean up the floor, please. Jayden, you keep eating."

Jayden shoved an entire stalk of broccoli in his mouth, chewing dramatically.

"Did you want a beer, babe? I need a beer. There's an open red wine in there too."

"I'll have the red. Thank you. Jax, that's good enough. Hand that to Daddy and finish your dinner." God, he was ready to broil them both.

Early headed back to the kitchen, turning on the music on his way. Ah, the boys were getting their next warning sign that Daddy was about to stroke out.

"Both of you finish up. Jax? Broccoli. Now. And then upstairs for reading."

"Reading?" Jaxson started to whine, but his big brother gave him the elbow. "Okay. Reading."

"Thank you. Don't forget to tell your daddy thank you for the dinner, please? He made you chicken parm."

"Yes, sir. It was really good."

Connor watched as Early set down his wine. "Thanks, honey."

"Thankyoufordinnerdaddymaywepleasebe…" Jaxson took a deep breath. "'Scused?"

"It was so good, Daddy. Thank you."

"You're very welcome, sons. Please wash your hands after feeding/handling/touching the mouse in any way and before your reading." Early sat with his beer, waiting for the boys to leave. "I bet that mouse escapes and infests the house."

"I won't say I told you so." They'd had mice before; it was a thing. They'd just go to battle stations. "DEFCON 1." He looked his husband over critically. "Thank you for the wine. Something's wrong. What is it?" This was the part where the cowboy in Early won out first, and Early would say "I'm fine", until they were done with dishes or headed to bed and then he might sigh and fess up.

If it was really awful Early would find an excuse to go hide in the garage for a few minutes and *then* they'd talk.

"I'm fine. I—" Early twisted the top of his bottle. "It's just some bad news from my dad."

And then there was this scenario. "Oh, honey." He got up from his chair and pulled one closer to Early. "Not your Momma?" Please not his mother; she was the queen of amazing women.

"Fuck no. She's going to outlive us all. Uncle Rick. It won't be long now."

Early's Uncle Rick was one of Early's biggest supporters, a good, amazing man who had rapid-onset Alzheimer's. The last time they'd gone out for Easter, Rick had been violent, terrified, and restrained.

"You need to go. Why are you sitting here? When did you find out? Let's get you on a plane." He pulled out his phone.

"No. He's not there. Pop says he's not there at all. He had a stroke this morning, and they're just waiting for the end. Me being there won't help. I'll go afterward, when I can be useful."

"You're sure? I'm so sorry. You should have told me. I could have at least come home early, dealt with this lunacy." He leaned closer and kissed Early's cheek, then took a hand in his. "I know, it's not worth hashing out. I'm here now, though."

"Thanks, babe. I love you. I'm just tired."

Ha hated this for Early. Early was close with his parents, but Rick had been the first one in Early's corner, the first person Early really trusted with difficult things like how to manage being gay on a ranch.

"Go take a shower, put on comfy PJ's, and go to bed. I got the dishes. I didn't bring home any work tonight, so I'll join you as soon as I get the hooligans in bed." Early liked a back rub, and he had magic fingers. It was a gift.

"I'll deal with the dishes, babe. You handle Thing One and Thing Two." Early sighed and shook his head. "Lord have mercy, I hate this for him."

God, the man was impossible to pamper, even when he needed it. He ran a soothing hand over Early's shoulder and stood. "Rick was loved. If he can manage to remember anything, he'll remember that. Doesn't matter by who."

"I'll shoot myself first, before I let myself get there. I won't make you watch me become a...whatever Rick is now." Early's expression was pure horror, pure pain. "I don't understand how the good lord lets someone's brain dissolve in their damn skulls."

"Oh, Early." He caught his husband by the nape and pulled the cowboy into his arms. "It's going to be okay, honey. It's okay." God, he hoped so. Early was scaring him a little bit. "I love you."

"I love you." Early let him hold on, leaning in hard. "This is hard. I miss him."

"I know. I know it is. Just breathe and do what you need to do, okay?" He'd insist they go for the service. Bring the boys.

"Yeah. Yeah, we'll need to plan on going out for the funeral. I'm betting either Monday or Tuesday next week, if he dies during the night." Early took a hitching breath. "I need to go. Do you—we haven't ever talked about how to do funerals with the boys. How do you feel?"

"I think this was someone very important to you, and the kids should be there."

"Can you come? I can't—I can't do this and deal with them alone."

"Of course I'll come. I'm not going to let you do this by yourself. We'll all go." He had to be there; where else would he be? Early and their boys were all the family he had.

It was a six-hour drive to Durango, but it was a beautiful ride, and the boys were happy to have extra time on their games. They could head out Friday after school, have supper on the road, and get themselves a hotel. Early's folks had sold their home and bought a two-bedroom condo, and while it was a lovely place, it was about two thousand square feet too small for their sons.

He could keep them busy while Early talked with his parents. Board games, cards...

Okay, their Switches. Or Benadryl.

"You're not alone, honey."

"No." Early kissed his jaw. "Not since I picked up this guy at a little dive bar."

"I've never set foot in a dive bar. I'm way too classy." It had definitely been a dive bar. But he'd never admitted it before, so why start now?

"Mmhmm. Dive bar. Neon lights. Scary bathroom. Shots of tequila."

"Tequila and neon, sure. I don't believe I used the bathroom. A sports bar maybe." He flirted, playing Early's game.

"There was a TV, I think...and a piece of shit pool table."

"The hottest man on earth was playing pool." And losing, but the table had been warped and the felt was bunched up near one of the side pockets. It'd looked like a neglected mini-golf course. He hadn't cared if Early had won or lost, he'd just been watching.

"Eh, I saw you, and it was over. I never saw another man." Early said the words like they were simply a fact, just something that was an unalienable truth.

"Doesn't make it a dive bar." He took a kiss and brought the last of the dishes into the kitchen.

"Dive. Deep dive. Like one of them submarines."

Connor laughed. He couldn't help it. "That's a new one. I like it."

Early bowed deeply. "Well, thank you, sir. I worked hard for it."

They loaded the dishwasher, moving around each other easily. Early should have gone up to bed, but he didn't go, he waited and helped until everything was done, and the house was locked up and quiet. Maybe his man just didn't want to be alone. He could understand that.

"You sure you don't want to shower while I tuck the boys in?"

"Join me after?" Early still looked a little shell-shocked, stressed out, with red-rimmed eyes and tight lips.

"Yeah. I'm all yours tonight. Promise." He gave Early another kiss, wondering how Early had hidden this so well from him until dinner and marveling how quickly his husband was falling apart now that that burden was off his shoulders. "I won't be long." He followed Early up the stairs toward the kids and the bedroom.

"Sounds good to me." Early tugged his shirt up and off as he walked. "Y'all sleep good, boys. I love you."

"Night, Daddy!" Jayden called, while Jaxon's greeting was totally muffled. Possibly because Jayden was trying to smother him with a pillow.

He could see Early's shoulders slumping as he disappeared into the bedroom.

2

Early grabbed the phone as soon as it lit up. He'd turned off the sound so it wouldn't wake anyone, and god knew he hadn't been sleeping, so he saw it immediately and slipped from the bed and down the stairs to answer his dad. "Hey, old man. It over?"

There was a hefty sigh, and then his dad said, "Yes, thank god. He didn't go easy, but when the good lord came for him, he had a look of peace on him. I'll take it."

"I'm sorry. This sucks."

"Me too, but it was time. He was lost in his own mind, and he was scared. It was no way to go."

"No, sir. When you need me to come?"

"Can you come out by this weekend? We'll bury him Monday, I imagine. I've already spoken to Jacob, and he's going to do the service for us at the church. All the details were dealt with before Rick got too sick to make them."

He nodded, making notes on the notebook that lived in the little basket with cards and keys and change. "We'll be there. I'll grab a hotel room for the kids."

"Just stay at Rick's, son. It's clean, and Momma says she'll buy y'all a bill of groceries." Pop sounded so goddamn tired. "It'll be a hard week, yessir."

Oh, man. It would be weird to stay at Rick's, but the place was a damn mansion, not to mention beautiful. "You sure that's... I don't know, appropriate?"

"He loved you like you were his own. He'd want you there."

He closed his eyes, refusing to cry. If he was a believer—and he was—then he had to believe that Rick was in a better place, where his pain was over. That was nothing to wail about. "All right. Do you need anything? Like right now, I mean?"

"Nah. I'm going to bed. I'm pondering sleeping for three days. Call me tomorrow with times and such, okay?"

"Will do. Love you, Pop."

"I love you more. Night, son."

Early hung up and made himself a cup of coffee, knowing he wasn't heading back to bed.

He watched it brew and had just taken his first eye-opening sip when Connor wandered in wearing slippers and a thick robe. "Too early for coffee," Connor mumbled and walked right up to lean in. "Can't sleep?"

"Pop called. It's over." It was never too early for coffee.

"Oh. I'm sorry. But it's cold, honey. Come on back to bed." Connor's hand slipped into his.

He wasn't going to be able to sleep, but he could play Candy Crush and drink coffee and relax. "All right. We can do that."

"Good. We can stoke up the fire when we get up there." Connor led him upstairs. "Do you want to leave as soon as they're done with school? I'll take the day off and pack us all up."

"It's up to you, love. You'll need Friday, Monday and

Tuesday at the least. Can you take Thursday too?" God, that would be good, to have another set of hands, someone to be there to make noise.

"Honey, I'll take the week. Okay? I can get a couple of hours in there if I need to, I'll just bring my laptop. We'll tell the kids' teachers."

"Thank you." He put his coffee on the bedside table and grabbed Connor's hand, holding on.

Connor fussed over him, helping him back into bed, getting them settled together so he could lie on Connor's chest. "There, now." Connor pulled the blankets back up, warming them both. "We don't have to sleep; we can just be here. Okay? Together?"

"Yeah. Pop sounded wrecked. He wants us to stay at Rick's with the boys." Was that okay? Was that good with Connor?

"Whoa, that's kind of...weird, isn't it? To stay...what did you tell him?"

He couldn't help but chuckle, tickled to death. "I said it was weird."

Connor's chest vibrated and his abs jumped with the giggles. "But we're doing it anyway, aren't we?"

"I guess so, yeah. I can get with Demming about the ranch details while we're there." Demming had been Uncle Rick's lover once upon a time and had been the ranch manager for decades.

"I haven't met Demming, have I? He always seemed like a busy guy. That'll be good I guess." Connor's fingers slid through his hair and rubbed his nape. His husband loved to touch.

"You've seen him at Christmas and all. He's quiet, but you liked him well enough." Demming was a master at blending.

"Wow, okay. Well, I'll pay better attention?" Connor sighed. "Okay so we're staying in a...haunted house. Got it. Are you okay? Tell me what's on your mind. I know who he was to you, hon."

"I'm just tired. It breaks my heart that he died so hard, but I know he has to be at peace now. I'm not sure what I'm going to tell the boys, but they're going to have to love on their Papaw pretty hard."

"You just tell them that. That your dad is sad because he lost his older brother and needs extra love and lots of help. Hell, you need some extra love too."

"Yeah." Part of him wanted to tell Pop the kids were sick, the car had problems, they couldn't come, but that was the bullshit coward's way out, and he wouldn't take it, dammit.

"Don't worry, the kids always make your parents happy. They love the boys. Just having them there will be good for them."

"True that." He had to grin. His folks had fussed when he'd come out of the closet, not because he was gay, but because they weren't going to have grandbabies. But Connor was determined to make it happen, and it was one of the reasons he knew they were meant for each other. He hadn't been sure he was destined to be a father, but Connor showed him he was.

And now they had two of the wildest amazing monkeys in the world.

Connor sighed heavily. "What are we going to do with the damn mouse?"

"Let it go? See if Janey next door will watch it?"

"I'm not sending a wild mouse to Janey. We're going to have to let it go. He's going to be so mad." Connor chuckled. "Well, let him be mad at me. I'll take this one."

"They're old enough to have a dog. When we get home, maybe we should get them a puppy." Boys needed dogs.

Connor hummed. "Perfect. Maybe two. You're really not going back to sleep are you?"

"I don't know. Probably not. You never know with me." He kissed Connor's chin.

"You want a blowjob?" By Connor's tone, he should have guessed that was coming. "I might know how to do one of those."

"You might, huh?" He cracked up, because his husband, as stressful as life was, did make him laugh. "I might be addicted to your mouth."

"I think?" Connor rolled them so he was on his back. "Can I try? I wanna try." A hot tongue that knew damn well what it was doing tasted a nipple, then lapped at his sternum. "Could be fun."

"You're a bad man." But his prick started paying attention, didn't it? Hell yes it did.

"You're my stunningly hot husband." Connor wiggled his PJ's down just enough that he could feel the cool air on his prick.

"Yes, sir. All yours." His eyelids went heavy, and he spread for Connor.

"Mmm. That's my man." Connor started slow, letting him slide past those hungry lips and then pop back out again, fingers tugging and stroking his balls. Little things that demanded his attention.

It was so easy to let himself relax, let himself feel every second of Connor's focus. He braced himself on the mattress, his bent legs cradling Connor.

"Mmm." Connor hummed around him, then took his cock in deep and did it again, making his toes curl. "Love your cock," Connor said when he pulled up again, and followed that by tracing the line through the tip with his tongue. "Taste so good."

His answer was a whimper and a soft, needy shiver. He never had been able to refuse Connor anything. Ever.

Connor didn't say anything more, just repeated that move again and again, humming, driving his tongue around the head and taking him in deep like his only purpose was to drive Early out of his mind.

He pushed up onto his elbows, needing to see this, to watch that dark head bob. His husband was focused and enjoying himself, which only made the whole thing hotter. Every so often Connor would let him go to nuzzle his balls or stroke the sensitive skin behind them, throwing off the rhythm and distracting him again.

"Love you," he groaned, his eyes rolling. "Love you so goddamn much."

Connor hummed in response, then swallowed around his prick, over and over.

"Oh fuck. Gonna..." The threat was too late, because it was all over but the crying.

Connor brought him down easy with lots of soft sounds and gentle touches, finally climbing back up to kiss him and share his pillow. "My cowboy. So fucking pretty."

"Yours." He curled in, soaking up Connor's heat. "Hold me, please?"

"You know it." Connor's solid arms went around him and held on. "I'm right here. You're going to be okay."

"I am. He's in a better place. He's home and in his right mind." And he had faith in that. He had to.

"Try to sleep. Tomorrow is going to be a long day—the drive, the kids, the grandparents..."

"Mmhmm. After school." He nuzzled closer, sinking into

the sound of Connor's heartbeat. "Love you. Gonna make it."

"We got this far. Odds are pretty damn good, honey." Connor's breathing was sure and even, his heartbeat strong and reassuring.

He kissed Connor's jaw and then dissolved, sinking into sleep.

3

Connor was pretty sure he'd slept, but he didn't feel like it. It was a strange bed in a strange house that belonged to a dead man and that all added up to serious weirdness. He didn't know how the heat worked, if there was any, but they'd packed coffee so he started by making a pot and tugging his robe tighter around him while it brewed.

In true control-what-you-can fashion, Early had insisted on driving the whole way, all six-plus hours, and they'd driven straight through to Durango without stopping so the kids would sleep. That seemed to have worn the man out a bit, so Connor hoped Early had gotten a little sleep too.

He looked out the window over the kitchen sink and he could see part of a barn, some fencing and animals he wasn't going to come close to identifying without his contacts. Cows maybe. Horses possibly. Or, knowing Rick, they could be llamas or alpacas.

Something split off from the animals and moved closer. It was wearing a cowboy hat, which was unusual for a cow. The thought occurred to him that he might be seeing ghosts, but that was too creepy for before coffee, so he decided it must be Demming.

Early came padding through a dark, wood-framed door in a pair of jeans and a sweatshirt. "Need to pop up the heater, huh?"

Connor hadn't ever seen so much wood. Ever. Every single room in this huge place was raw wood, huge logs crossed the ceiling, even the bathrooms were all wood. The only things that weren't were the kitchen and bathroom counters, which were stone. He couldn't imagine the amount of work that went into a place like this.

"I guess. The kids will complain when they wake up. Do you know how? There's coffee. Also, there's a cowboy in the yard."

"Demming. He'll be up for coffee, no doubt. And the thermostat's in the hallway. I'll start a fire when I know we'll be here for more than an hour."

"I better get dressed." He slipped his arms around Early and kissed him. "Demming shouldn't see me in my robe."

"He's seen me in way less, but this is mine to gaze upon, hmm?" Early grabbed his ass and squeezed. "I need to find out what's what, you know? I'm assuming all this is going to Pop, but I don't know. We might be staying in Demming's house."

"Oh, geez. Well I don't want to be half naked in Demming's house either." He grinned and hurried off, finding jeans and a sweater in his suitcase and dropping in his contacts. He needed to know what animals were out there. By the time he was back in the kitchen, Early was cooking breakfast. He had the best husband in the universe.

"Daddy! Can we have a fire?"

"Daddy! Can we ride a horse?"

"Daddy! When is Papaw coming over? Is Mamaw coming too?"

"Daddy!"

"Daddy!"

"Daddy!"

Early just let it all flow over him and kept making sausage and biscuits.

"Boys. Why does it sound like there are four of you in here instead of two? Sit down. At the table." He started herding, and there might as well have been four of them. They were so excited to be here, excited to see their grandparents. "Sit."

"Daddy's making sausage!" Jaxson explained, like he hadn't noticed. "And there's biscuits."

"And he says if we're super good, we can go on the train!" Jayden joined in.

"Well, Daddy is in charge here, so if he says so, then I'd think about being super good. Starting now."

Jayden sat and scooted his chair in, and his brother followed.

Go Daddy.

"You guys want some juice? I saw some in the fridge." Early's mom must have done a little shopping for them.

"Yes, please!"

Ooh. A "please." Score.

He needed coffee.

"Your coffee's all fixed, babe." Early handed him a mug with a dollop of sweet cream in it, offering him a wink. "I invited Demming for breakfast. He's finishing the feeding and all."

Then his cowboy was on the move, getting five juice glasses down.

"Poor guy. He's in for it." Connor chuckled and sipped

his coffee, which was perfect, of course. "You found the thermostat at least." He wandered over to the kitchen window to figure out what he'd seen earlier. "Oh, that's just a pony. I thought it was a cow without my contacts. What else is out there?"

"Oh, there's about a hundred head of cattle, two dozen horses, four donkeys, ten alpacas, and chickens. Lots of chickens."

"Oh, Jesus. That's...busy."

"Chickens!" Jayden shouted, and he was instantly sorry he'd asked.

"Bawk!"

"Bawk bwawk!"

He sipped his coffee and pretended he didn't hear. It had worked for Early.

"I'll introduce you, but, if you scare them and the hens stop laying, then they'll become fried chicken..."

Oh, that was evil.

"I like fried chicken," Jayden added helpfully.

"Noooooo!" Jaxson wailed. "You're so mean! We have to be nice to the chickens."

Jayden chuckled. "Okay, I like eggs too. Geez."

"Nice is the way to be, boys." Early winked at Connor. "We're going to meet up with the folks at noon, see what we need to do."

"Okay." He sipped his coffee. He felt like he was going to need it. He liked Early's parents, his mother especially. Mr. Jericho—Wyatt—was kind, but he was the stoic cowboy type and happiest sitting on the porch and talking about the weather, or about nothing at all. It had taken Connor a long time to understand and follow Early's advice to just sit and let the silence be. It was still difficult; he was used to big city small talk, but he did it now, and it did pay off. "It's going to be a tough day. I'll wrangle the boys as much as I can so you don't have to."

"Thank you. Momma's going to want to take them to buy clothes for the funeral, get them haircuts, and all." Early rolled his eyes. "Like we didn't manage."

Early had brought them all starched jeans, black button-downs, and boots, then the adults had Stetsons, bolo ties, and Western-cut jackets in a deep gray. It was a sad occasion, but he didn't mind dressing like a cowboy. He always looked fantastic.

"Well, you know, what do men know about clothing?" He grinned at Early. "And the boys' hair is always too long. Every time we come down here."

"Always. We can't be trusted, you know."

He always said the same thing to Momma. *We haven't starved them or lost them yet, so we're doing all right.* That got him the eye roll. He got that a lot. "Someday I'm going to shave their heads the day before we get here."

"She'd be so pleased, and then she'd worry that they had lice, and we didn't want her to know." Early was barely keeping the chuckles at bay.

"Damn. We really can't be trusted. Who raised me? Yankee chimpanzees?" He gave in and giggled his way back to the coffee pot.

"Well...you do have to wax your butt..." Early managed to say that without moving his lips.

He was about to shoot back with something sarcastic but was reminded there were children in the room.

"Dad waxes his butt?" Jayden blurted out.

"What is waxing?" Jaxson asked.

"I don't wax my butt." He poured himself a second cup of coffee without turning around. "All yours, Daddy."

"I was teasing him, boys. Waxing is when you rip your

hair out on purpose. Can y'all imagine your father doing that?"

Jaxson's eyes went wide. "No way."

"Nope. Dad is not into pain. He hates having a hangnail," Jayden announced, and Jaxson stared at his brother.

"What's a hanged nail?"

Dad isn't into pain? Was this a real conversation? "It's these little pieces of fingernail that grow away from your finger. And sometimes they hurt, and no one likes having them. You boys need to stop yammering and eat." There was not enough coffee in Colorado for him this morning.

Jayden leaned over the table toward Jaxson. "I bet we go to the candy store after our haircuts."

Jaxson's eyes lit up. "Oh yeah!"

Early fixed them with a look. "Just remember if you act like hooligans, your granny will fuss at me, and—"

"Poop rolls downhill!" they dutifully responded.

"And y'all are at the bottom."

He cracked up. "Eat! Good grief." He pulled out a plate for himself and handed it to Early.

There was a quiet knock at the door, and he waved through the window. "Come in, Demming."

"You make gravy, Sonny Jim?"

"Yessir. Come on in and fix you a plate."

Demming smiled at Early, the man's eyes shimmering with unshed tears. "It's like seeing your uncle standing there at the stove."

He took his plate from Early and set it down with the boys. "Would you like some coffee? How do you take it?"

"Black, please. Boys, how are you?"

The kids looked to him for their clues. This was the first

death in the family, and honestly, they hadn't seen Rick in a few years, so he was like a myth.

He gave them a nod and a wink. "We got in late last night; we're all a little bleary-eyed this morning. Say hello to Mr. Demming, boys."

"Hello, Mr. Demming," they said in unison.

"Are you having breakfast with us? Daddy has biscuits."

"And gravy."

"And Mamaw bought orange juice."

That's it, boys. He poured Demming a mug of coffee.

"She's a queen among women. She taught your daddy how to make biscuits. Did you know that?"

"Uh-huh. Mamaw loves to cook. She makes chocolate chip cookies not from a box." Jaxson's eyes were wide, like that was a miracle.

"You take a shortcut one time..." He grinned and set Demming's coffee down by an empty chair. "Warm out, huh?"

"For April? It is. Going to be a nice summer. I foresee a lot of calves, and a foal or two."

"That should keep you busy." He pulled out the chair so Demming could sit with his plate, and then joined them. "Do you have much help?"

"No, I'm on my own. I'm hoping Rick set something up for me." Demming dug into the biscuits and gravy, moaning low. "Man, you get to eat like this a lot?"

"Every weekend. And lots of dinners. Early's a really good cook."

"Daddy does all the cooking because Dad goes to work *every day*."

"Every day. Like school. Every-every day."

He chuckled. "I think Mr. Demming gets it."

"Daddy doesn't hafta work. He's a stay-at-home momma-daddy."

Oh boy. He didn't know how his husband was going to take that one. He glanced over his shoulder at Early. "Are you coming to sit, honey?"

"I am." Early didn't respond to the boys, just sat with them and drank his coffee. "We're going to be heading over to deal with things, and let the boys hang with my momma. You need anything from town?"

"No, I'm fine, thank you. Plenty to do around here. It's good that you're here for them though."

"Wouldn't be anywhere else. I'll be back to help this evening, and you can let me know what you need from me." Early offered Demming a tired smile. "I'm going to have to know which horse we're riding his boots out on."

Demming gave him a short nod. "Bucky, I think. Rick was the last one to ride the old man before we turned him out. I'll clean him up today."

"Okay. Good deal. Thank you." Early nodded once. "Uncle Rick would be pleased as all get out."

"He would." Demming cleared his throat, finished off his coffee and stood. "I better get back at it." Demming dropped a hand to Early's shoulder. "Let's take a walk, you and me, sometime before you head back up to Denver."

"You know it. I'll be here until the reading of the will, one way or the other. We'll chat."

"Thank you for breakfast, that was a treat." Demming gave him and the boys a wave and slipped out the kitchen door.

"Who is he, Daddy?"

"He's Uncle Rick's foreman. He runs the ranch. This place is too big for one man, you know?" Early picked his biscuit apart. "Uncle Rick said this house was built in the Seventies, huh? That's why there's all the bare wood."

"It's pretty amazing."

"It's kind of old, isn't it?" Jayden shrugged.

"It is. That's why it's so amazing. This is a one-of-a-kind place. Eight bedrooms, eight baths, hot tub. I used to love the guest house. I pretended it was mine when I was a little boy."

Eight bedrooms was huge. "I don't know how you take care of a place like this. Demming can't do it alone that's for sure."

Jaxson got up with his plate, and Early pointed to the sink. "Scrape your plates, dishes in the sink please. And then go wash up. Clean hands, clean faces."

"Yes, sir, Mister Daddy, sir!" Jayden saluted, and the boys were off and running, so excited to explore.

"I'll do the dishes real quick, and we'll load up." Early kissed his cheek.

"I can help, you cooked." He scooped up dishes and took them to the sink, then started to clean out the coffee maker. "You okay?"

"As okay as I can be, I guess. I'm not looking forward to this next bit, but—like everything else, it'll heal." Early sighed softly and shook his head.

"Just take it a day at a time, right?" Connor kissed Early's shoulder, then took a dishtowel out of a drawer. He'd only been here a handful of times, but nothing changed about this place. He knew where everything was. "We've got this."

"We do. I want to show the boys all around before we go home. Show them the guest house, the barns?"

"Of course. They'd love that. We have plenty of time." And once the house moved on to someone else, it was hard to know if they'd be staying here again or not. He finished drying dishes while Early put them away and the kitchen was spotless in no time.

"Thank you, babe. I'm glad you're here. Seriously." Early pulled him into a kiss.

He gave back as good as he got. Early was always beautiful to him, whether he was doing dishes or in bed. "I love you, cowboy I wouldn't be anywhere else."

"I know. I'm a lucky fucker." Early's smile warmed him up. "I'll buy you jalapeno poppers at the brewpub this afternoon."

"Oh, now you've made the trip worth it." He gave Early a wink as the boys came rushing back in. "Let's see." He inspected hands. "Teeth all brushed?"

"Yes, Dad."

"Clean undies."

"Dad! Duh!"

"Duh, huh?" There was never enough underwear in the hamper.

Early chuckled and stomped into his boots, winking at him. "Hurry up, boys. I want to take you up to the magic balcony. You too. It's on the third floor."

He was ready. He helped the boys get their sneakers on and tied. "Okay, Daddy. Let's go."

They went to the second floor, and then to Rick's bedroom, where Early opened a secret pocket door. There were stairs leading up to the round room.

Oh, he'd never been up there.

"What is this?" He followed the kids up the stairs. "I thought this was decorative."

"Nope." The round room was a library, with books everywhere, floor to ceiling, with a big, overstuffed chair, and a huge balcony that looked out over the mountains. It stole his breath.

"Early, why have you never shown me this before?"

"Daddy, this is so cool!" Both kids ran for the door to the balcony.

"It was in Uncle Rick's room. It seemed inappropriate somehow. Boys, you be careful out there."

"Yes, sir!" The boys stepped outside, delighted by the view and the novelty of the balcony.

He slipped an arm around Early's hips. "You're right. This is pretty cool, though. Did he spend a lot of time up here?"

"He did. I used to hide up here for hours, watching the wild mustangs run."

"Wow, really?" He looked out the windows, imagining Early so young and hiding from the world. "You're a good man." He tugged his husband in for a kiss.

Early hummed and kissed him right back, the connection threatening to deepen until the cry of, "Daddy! Dad! Come and see!"

Early's smile as he rubbed their noses together was pure happiness. "Coming, boys."

They went out, and the view was stunning. Mountains in the back, huge barns with dark brown and black horses in the front. The cattle roamed in pods here and there, and farther back, near what looked like a river, a mass of animals ran like they were one.

"Sure is beautiful."

"Dad! Daddy! Look at the horses!"

"And the cows!"

"Mooooo."

"Mooo!"

Early's eyes were on the animals in the back. "Wild mustangs—the proof that there is a god and He loves us."

The expression on his husband's face was oddly... blissful.

"I thought that was mashed potatoes?" Sometimes it was coffee. He chuckled and hugged Early. "I don't think I've ever seen them before. There are so many."

"There's a main herd, and then two smaller ones. It'll be time to split them soon, so that they can thrive."

"Who does that?" Demming had his hands full with the ranch as it was.

"I—It's on my list to talk to Demming about, I guess." Early grabbed his phone and jotted some more notes. "You know my pop ain't interested in dealing with it, not right now."

"Daddy!" Jayden shook his head. "Isn't, not ain't."

Early chuckled and shook his head. "Sorry, son."

Oh good grief, Jayden knew better. "Jayden, don't correct your father. And *please* don't correct your grandparents."

"Yes, sir. Sorry, Daddy."

Early's list was so long it felt like they'd never be able to go home. "We better get going."

"I know. I just wanted to share this with all y'all. It's special." Early shook his head. "I don't know how I'll be able to know it's not in the family."

"I bet Rick left it to Demming, right? We can help him get someone to help here." He waved the boys back into the room. "Downstairs, guys."

"This is the coolest, Daddy!"

"Can I bungee jump from up here?"

Early's eyes went wide. "God no. Jaxson, downstairs. Now."

"That's your fault." He laughed and followed Early out, watching as he closed the hidden door. "That is pretty cool."

"It is. It's a hidden library. How many houses have a hidden library?"

"This is the only one I know of that's not in a book or a movie." And it was more than a library, it was an amazing place, Connor thought. "It must have been pretty cool growing up."

"It was. I spent so much time here, you know? Momma had her book tours in the summers, mostly, and Daddy went with her, but I wanted to be here with Uncle Rick, riding."

And Rick understood who Early was, which had to be good too. God, this had to be so hard on his husband. "I'm glad you have those memories."

They went out to the truck, and Connor breathed in the clean air. It was lovely here. He hoped that Rick had made arrangements that would keep it in Early's life. That was obviously on Early's mind too.

He supposed they'd find out soon enough.

4

They all headed into Durango, the boys choosing the music, one song after another. It was a lovely drive into the valley, with the town appearing as they followed the river in.

Early's folks lived in a condo on the New Mexico side of the city, and they had to go through everything to get there. It was tiny compared to Denver, just a silly little mountain town, but full of life and outdoor fun.

He'd loved it here, and he had a thousand silly stories, but they weren't something that fit in his life in Denver with Connor. He'd gone to CMC with the intention of coming home and doing research, but there wasn't a huge call for hydrologists in the city.

"Are we almost there?"

"Soon, buddy. This place hasn't changed much, huh?"

"No, but that's cool. I want to go rafting again. That was so much fun!"

Yeah, and Connor had damn near died.

"We'll see, son. It's still too damn cold."

"Ah, rafting. Not really my sport." Connor snorted. "I'd try it again, though."

"It was best when you almost fell in the water and Daddy grabbed you." Jaxson's giggles filled the cab.

"Yes, Daddy was my brave, strong hero." And he'd gotten a nice blowjob in the guest room as a thank-you that night. "You nearly destroyed that pillow," Connor whispered.

"Mmhmm..." He reached over and squeezed Connor's thigh. God, he loved the feel of that lean muscle under the denim.

Connor covered his hand and held it. "So your momma will disappear with the kids, you'll sit with your dad, and ... where do you want me? I can just turn on a game until you need me."

Honestly? He wanted Connor with him. Everything felt off and weird and—uncomfortable. Like he was wearing underwear that weren't his. All his bits were covered, but it wasn't right.

Connor had always been so good at reading him. "Or I can hang out with you and your dad...?"

"Yeah? Maybe, until we figure out what he wants from me, exactly." Because he knew that there was something—he just knew it.

"I've got your back. No worries. Whatever he needs, we'll just listen and make it happen."

"Right. I hope we—" He didn't even know how to finish that sentence. He didn't know what he wanted. It was killing him to think about losing the ranch, but he knew, no question, that there was no way his dad could handle it, and for all his momma was a Colorado girl now, she was...not a rancher. Skiing? Yes. Rafting? Yes. Kayaking, biking, hiking, snowboarding—yes to all of it.

No critters.

"Me too." Connor squeezed his hand. "Hey, we're here, guys."

"Yay!" the boys shouted from the back seat.

"Oh boy. Here we go." Connor shook his head, grinning.

"Listen to me, no messing up your mamaw's house, okay? You behave, and we'll go on the train while we're here." The boys still talked about their last ride with the historic steam engine.

The boys both nodded. It wasn't that Momma was mean; she was just...fastidious, and she believed that little boys were just a touch horrifying.

He'd been a hooligan and a half, taking after his Uncle Rick in more ways than one.

"Good boys." Connor leaned over and kissed his cheek. "Let's go." Connor slid out of the truck and helped the boys down while he went and knocked on the front door.

"You don't have to knock, son." Momma opened the door and grabbed him, and he was always surprised that she didn't look like he remembered from when he was eighteen and left home. She was leaner now, and her long hair was silvery in between the dark. "You brought me all my favorite people."

"I did. How's it going?" *How's Daddy?*

"Busy. Stressed, but Richard was so careful to make sure everything was arranged."

"Mamaw!" Jayden and Jaxson scooted around him and hugged her, one on each side.

"My goodness, look at these boys. They're getting so tall." She hugged them back, smiling.

"We missed you," Jayden said, and Jaxson followed with, "We love you."

Momma just melted. Excellent job.

Connor's hand slipped into his, so proud.

"Come in, come inside, everyone. You too, Connor. You're looking well."

"Hello, Momma. Thank you. I love how you've done your hair." Connor kissed her cheek.

"Thank you. I'm going au natural. Wyatt likes it."

Early managed not to roll his eyes. His dad would love anything she did. Anything.

"I can see why."

Momma chuckled. "Charmer. I made cookies."

"Did you make your snickerdoodles?" Connor was a fan.

"Chocolate chip for the boys and snickerdoodles for your sweet tooth, yes."

"Chocolate chip?" Jaxson's eyes lit up.

Momma looked at him meaningfully. "Your father's in the den. Why don't you go on in and say hello. I'll get the boys a snack."

"Yes, ma'am." He shot Connor a smile and headed into the condo. "Hey, old man."

His dad stood up and offered him half of a smile. "Early. Lord, you're a sight for sore eyes."

"It's good to see you too." They shook hands before they sat. "How you doing?"

"I'm as well as could be expected. Real tired. Relieved a bit, because he needed to go on."

Early nodded, because he got it, or he guessed he did. Daddy'd had to be here and deal with shit. "Yessir. He's in a better place."

"So sorry for your loss." Connor sat beside him, close enough that he could feel the support.

"Thank you, Connor. Thanks for coming out. I appreciate it."

He grinned at his husband. That was a speech, from his dad.

Connor gave his knee a squeeze and Daddy got a nod. "Of course. That's what family does. It was important to Early to come for the service, and when he could be useful."

"Yes. I—Yes. We'll have the service Monday." His dad seemed so...lost. "I have his will, too."

"Okay..." That was a weird segue.

Connor leaned a little closer to Daddy. "You should let us know what we can do. We can take some of the arrangements and things off your hands, if you like. So you can relax a little."

"He's at the funeral home. Everything's been paid for. We just have to show up at the church."

"Did he leave the ranch to Demming?" That was the most fair, right?

"No."

Dammit. "Are you going to sell it, then?"

Momma wasn't moving. There was no way.

Daddy shook his head, expression serious as a heart attack. "It's not mine to sell, son."

He frowned, shocked as all get out. "Then who?"

Connor nodded like he understood something and spoke softly. "He left it to Early."

Daddy nodded. "That he did, Connor."

His heart stopped. "What?"

"The ranch, the house, the acreage. He said no one loved it like you did, and you were raised to take over."

He was going to pass out. Seriously. He was going to just pass right out.

"I started to see it this morning, when Demming was talking. I wondered." Connor rubbed his back with a firm hand. "You okay?"

Was he okay?

Fuck no. No, he wasn't okay. Early wasn't ever going to be

okay. How was he... How could he walk away from this and go back to Denver? More importantly, how could he ask Connor to come here? "I'm good. I wasn't expecting that."

"No, me either, but looking at it now, we probably should have been." Connor leaned back in his seat. "Is Demming going to be upset, Dad? Does he know?"

"He does. He was all over it. Rick left him a nice chunk of cash, and he loves his job. He's—he's going to head to California sooner than later, I think."

"California?"

"His daughter and grandbabies are there."

"Hm. That's...good for him." Connor cleared his throat and stood. "I'm going to see if there's coffee. Would anyone like some coffee?"

He shook his head, but his dad nodded. "Please."

As soon as Connor escaped, Pop leaned forward. "You okay, son?"

"I don't know. Jesus. The ranch? Me? No one was going to warn me? I mean, *Jesus!*" Someone should have warned him, dammit.

"I was sure you'd see it. Demming's close to retirement, and I'm...too old for ranching. Who did you think would be able to run it? You're the natural choice, and you're who he wanted. Rick wanted that place to be yours. He told me so a million times."

"Daddy, what am I going to do? Connor... The boys..." God, the boys would love it as much as he did.

"It's a big, wonderful place, son. But I can't tell you what to do. I can see it's going to be complicated and you're just going to have to make some choices."

He whispered low. "I've wanted to live there my whole life."

How was he going to be able to walk away?

"I know. So did Rick. You're a cowboy."

"Momma left a pot of coffee and a note. She's taken the boys shopping." Connor came back in with two mugs of coffee and handed one to Daddy.

"She's just looking for an excuse to spoil them." Daddy chuckled.

"Of course she is." She didn't want to be here for this conversation, and Early knew it.

Daddy sighed. "Well, I think I'm going to take my coffee and the paper and have a little lie down. It's been quite a day."

And that was Daddy escaping now. Dammit.

"It's not even noon, Daddy."

"I know."

Dammit. Early stared at his husband. "He left me the ranch."

"I heard." Connor held out his hand, offering him a cookie. "Snickerdoodle?"

So... Early now owned a ranch.

The thought that Rick might leave it to Early had occurred to Connor just that morning, but he'd decided to keep it to himself. On the face of it, this was a good thing. Early loved that place, had many happy memories there, and from what he could tell, Early actually wanted it.

So Connor was trying not to panic, because the reality of owning it was far more complicated than just loving it.

Early couldn't run a ranch from a house in Denver. Period. With some work, he could hire people, he could turn it into a self-sustaining operation, sure. But Connor had seen the look in his husband's eyes as he watched those mustangs run, and he knew Early wasn't going to want to trust it to someone else.

He knew it as well as he knew Early.

He also knew Early was as stunned as he was, probably more, and he was going to have to tread carefully.

"Momma makes good coffee," he said, totally avoiding the subject, and stuffed a cookie in his mouth so he couldn't say anything more than that. This whole situation had been engineered to drop the bomb in their laps and leave them to it.

"She does." Early stared at Connor's mug. "He left me the ranch. Three hundred acres plus the BLM lease for the mustang project. A five thousand square foot house, a guest house, a foreman's house, fishing pond, two horse barns, feed barn, tool shed..."

"It's a lot." Connor let the words just hang between them for a moment and took a sip of his coffee. It was a lot. A huge ranch and tons of land, the Bureau of Land Management lease, the livestock, other houses...it was overwhelming, in fact. He couldn't get his head around it. "It's a lot to...think about."

"Yeah. I don't know how to even start." Connor had no doubt that Early was telling the truth. Those eyes were wide and shocked and stunned.

He took a deep breath, set his coffee down and stepped closer to Early, trying to pull his gaze, get his attention. "Hey. What do you need from me?"

"I don't know. I don't even know how to figure that out. I thought I was coming to bury my uncle, not...this."

"Okay." Early needed some time to process this and the burial and everything else. They both did. "So, I'm just going to say this. I love you. And whatever comes next, we're going to figure it out together. Okay?" He didn't know what that meant, or where the compromise was yet, but there had to be one. He and Early were partners. "We're a team, right?"

"Yes. We're more than a team. We're a family." Early came to sit next to him. "I'm just shocked. Maybe someone should have mentioned it before now."

Someone should have. Perhaps Rick should have while he was still of sound mind. But it didn't seem like Demming had known either, so Rick had kept those cards close for some reason. "Probably they should have, but they didn't. I'm sure everyone felt they were doing the right thing, and given that they have all deserted us here alone after delivering the news, they obviously understand the situation it's put us in."

"Yeah. Yeah. Fuck..." Early stood and started pacing, quick, staccato steps that screamed worry.

He let Early pace for a minute or so, watching to see if it was helping. It wasn't. "Talk, honey. Off the top of your head, just say what's on your mind." As if he didn't know. As if he didn't have the same worries. But Early seemed like he might explode if he didn't let some of it out.

"I'm scared." The words burst out, as bald and raw as he'd ever heard, barring that first, "I love you," and, "I want kids."

He barely resisted the urge to hop up and put his arms around Early. It was hard to get his cowboy talking, and he needed to listen. "What scares you most?"

"Losing? Making bad decisions? Doing something stupid?" He tugged at his short, short hair. "Doing something I'll regret?"

"We're not going to sell it." He said that softly, trying to bring the energy down a little. "I promise."

"No? It's... I don't have words for what it is to me, what it means."

"You don't need words, Early. I can see it. I can feel it. I listen, honey. I know."

"So what? What do we do? How do we even begin to do this? The boys have to be back at school. You have to be back to work. I ha—There's so much to do."

"I don't know yet. We have a little time to think about it, right? It's not like Rick has been helping with the ranch lately. Demming is okay for a minute." He thought he did know though; he just didn't like the answer.

"Yeah. Yeah, I'll have to have a meeting with Demming, ask him where we are, what the money situation is." Early shook his head and sighed. "Christ, what a mindfuck."

He got up and slipped his arms around Early's waist. "We'll figure it out. There will be no bad decisions; you won't lose anything. There has to be a solution. We're smart, we'll find it."

He really hoped all of that was true. They'd make it true somehow, they had to. But it was what Early needed to hear right now.

Early leaned into him. "Damn, honey. I do love you. I'm so sorry about this craziness."

"Your family does know how to bring it, huh?" Connor chuckled softly. The boys were their own kind of chaos, but that was usually more...manageable. "It's kind of exhausting."

"It's maddening, but they're mine, right?" Early straightened up. "And I love them...usually."

"I know. Seems like they usually love you too." He hugged Early tight. "Feel better?"

"I feel shocked, but I'm not sure there's any way around that."

"Nope. There isn't. I think you should help your dad finish with the arrangements for Rick and put this aside until after the burial. For now, just trust that we'll figure it out. One thing at a time. We're here for a week." At least. He had a feeling Early would be here longer, but he was going to take his own advice and think about that later.

"Right. Let's get Uncle Rick settled, and the rest I can deal with in a bit." Early squeezed his fingers. "I don't like feeling this much, darlin'."

He hummed happily. He loved when Early called him darling. "I know." There was a time when big feelings had made Early go out to the garage and destroy something. Or burn something in the backyard. Anything but talk about it. He'd come by it honestly—noting that neither of his parents stuck around to talk about this. He'd come a long way. "You just inherited a ranch you've loved since you were a boy. It's a good thing. Above everything else, it's a good thing, honey."

Hopefully.

"Yeah. I—" Look at that wondering smile. It transformed Early into someone Connor wasn't sure he'd ever seen.

"That's better. That's my cowboy. Give me a kiss." He didn't wait, he just leaned right in. He definitely had misgivings and worries of his own about the ranch and no idea how they'd make it work, but his job right now was to be a good husband and get Early through a tough couple of days.

Then they'd decide what to do next. They had to.

5

"Amen." Early glanced at the boys, who studiously repeated after him.

They went to First UU in Denver, so the boys knew about all sorts of religions, traditions, and they were growing up to ask good questions, but this was their first funeral, and they were uncomfortable and a little wigged out. He could tell.

"Daddy? Do we have to go watch them bury him?" Jayden whispered. "Can't we just go have lunch?"

Early thought about that, but not for long. "Yes. Yes, we can. Let me talk to Papaw, and tell them we'll meet for lunch at the Taphouse, okay?"

Connor leaned closer. "You sure, honey? I can take them if you want to go."

"No. No, the boys are right. We've said goodbye. They've been amazing. Everyone will understand." He left the boys with Connor once the church started to empty out. "I'm taking the boys to lunch. They don't need to see a coffin in the ground."

"They've been very good. Even Momma said so." Daddy

winked at him, looking tired. "You go on, we'll see you there."

"Love you." He headed to the boys. "Come on, y'all. Let's go to the truck. Y'all can change out of the monkey suits in the back."

Jaxson giggled softly. "Ook ook ook."

"Everyone looks so nice though, I wish I could get a picture of us." Connor shrugged. "I guess that's not appropriate at a funeral."

"Probably not. And Jayden is already half naked..." Early snatched Jayden's clip-on tie out of the air as it went flying by.

"Well, you still look hot." Connor rested a hand on his thigh.

"Thank you. I'm in my Western best."

"It suits you. My handsome man."

"Ew," Jaxson complained from the back seat.

Jayden joined in. "Lalala. Yuck."

"One day, you'll be madly in love, and then I'll be teasing you two."

"Nope. I'm never going be gooey like you." Jayden said, nose wrinkling. "I'm going to be a batchedor."

"Is that some sort of dog, son?"

"It's when you don't want a...sniffigan other, Daddy!" Jayden sighed like they were the dumbest parents on earth.

Connor cracked up, just busted out laughing, doubled over in his seat. He was no help at all.

"Ah. Well, I am super lucky your dad decided to sniff me."

Jaxson didn't seem to follow at all. "You smell good, Daddy, don't worry."

Connor sat up, pink-faced and still giggling. "You smell great, I promise."

"Thank you both. I appreciate it. Irish Spring, Outlaw, and deodorant. It's a good mixture." Early managed a straight face, but he did it. Connor had given his Stetson cologne a nix about seventeen seconds into their love affair.

"Wow. Okay." Connor took a breath. "Are you two dressed?"

"Yes. Are we there yet? I'm *hungry*."

"Just about."

"I want waffles."

"Ooh. Waffles."

Connor's hand landed on his thigh again. "I don't know how you keep a straight face. I really don't."

"Hours of practice. I can't let them get to me, you know?" He winked over, tickled as all get out.

"It's a skill. I'm impressed. Handsome and brilliant. I am a lucky man." Connor was looking fine himself in the starched jeans and black shirt Early had packed for him. But then Connor looked good in just about anything.

In fact, he loved Connor in everything and nothing at all.

"Is this the place? We better get these guys some food before they get hangry." Connor was folding clothing as the boys handed him things.

"It is." The restaurant was big enough for lots of folks, the jalapeno toothpicks were amazing, and the beer was cold. He was a fan.

"We haven't been here before have we? I don't recognize it."

"It wasn't really little one friendly? I used to party here when I was a teenager."

Connor grinned at him. "Oh yeah? This should be fun. Everyone is going to know you, aren't they?" Connor helped the boys out of the truck.

"Some of them, sure. Maybe quite a few." He didn't

know, but he'd always had fun here, and Rick had been a regular.

The boys ran for the door and waited for them there, but Connor hung back with him, letting him lead. "And we're cool here? Or..."

"Uncle Rick had been having a threesome with the bartender and an electrician from the Four Corners, honey." He managed to say that with a straight face, just.

Connor shook his head, relaxing visibly. "The things a man doesn't know...in you go, guys."

"Early Jericho! Is that you?" A gorgeous dark-haired man stared at him, and it took him a second to recognize the guy he'd had a torrid affair with during the summer between high school and college.

"Jesus. Chayton? Chayton Benally?"

He got wrapped in a hard hug. "I heard your news. I wish your family peace."

"Thank you, Chay. God, it's been an eon."

Connor cleared his throat, and Early knew exactly what was up as Connor put on his most charming smile and offered Chay a hand. "Hi, I'm Connor."

"Chay, this is my husband, Connor, and our boys."

"No shit. Wow. Wow, he's hot, man. Good job."

Early nodded. He knew. He had picked a beautiful, strong, smart son of a bitch.

"Thank you." Connor never minded a compliment. "I think I did even better, though. Good to meet you."

"Same. Want to catch up later? I'm heading down to the river for the afternoon."

"I'm in town for another couple of days, for sure." And he thought he'd be turning around and coming right back.

"Good. You feed your crew. I'll text you later. Great to see you." Chay gave them both a nod and headed out.

"He's good-looking," Connor teased as they were seated.

"He is." And the man had gotten better looking as he got older. "He's ski patrol up at the mountain and a river guide in the summer, or at least he was, last I heard."

"Athletic too. I better keep my eye on you." Connor teased.

"They have buttermilk waffles and blueberry waffles and peanut butter waffles and chocolate chip waffles and banana waffles and apple waffles..."

"Blueberry! No, chocolate chip! No..."

"Boys. Behave. Think about what you want." Quietly. "If you want to get a couple kinds to share, you can."

The boys started conspiring softly.

"What are you having, honey?" Connor asked. "I'm actually pretty hungry too. I'm thinking about a burger. Or fried chicken."

"I want the jalapeno sticks and an order of the potato skins." Bacon and cheese and ranch—win, win, win.

"Ooh. Good call. I'm going to have the chicken. And a bite of yours. And a beer." Connor closed his menu. "Boys?"

"Blueberry and chocolate chip," they said at the same time.

"Sounds great."

"And a beer," Jayden added, giggling.

"Root beer it is!" He winked over at his root-beer-loving boy.

"Me too, Daddy?" Jaxson asked, then whispered low. "But white?"

"White beer it is." So two Fat Tires, a root beer, and a Sprite.

"I am told you're a VIP." Their waitress stepped up the table and smiled at Early. "I'm Lucy."

"Hey, Lucy. I'm Rick Jericho's nephew. We're celebrating his life today."

"There was a horse with his boots on it. Papaw *cried*." Jaxson's eyes went wide.

Lucy nodded at Jaxson. "That's a powerful message, right? It's good to cry when you're sad; it gets all the feelings out." She turned back to him. "I'm sorry for your loss. We all knew Rick well. He was one of the best ones."

"He was, thank you." He stood and shook her hand, then sat and ordered their drinks.

"Did everybody know Uncle Rick?" Jayden asked.

"Lots of folks did, yeah. Durango is a little town, and our family's been here a long time." Four generations they had been on the ranch. It was theirs.

"Does she know we want waffles?"

"She will. She's getting our *beers* first." Connor winked at him, approving.

"Oh. Cool. Cool. So...is Uncle Rick still in that box? I mean, is he going to rot?"

Early tried not to wince at the question, but he wasn't going to not answer. "His body is in the coffin, yes. But his soul isn't there. The part of him that was real and special and loving—that's not in there. I think Uncle Rick's soul is in heaven."

"They'll bury his body in a nice spot where people can visit and read his headstone to remember him."

"So Papaw can visit if he wants to."

"Yes, exactly."

The drinks arrived, which was good timing. "What are we eating, folks?"

"Waffles!"

"Blueberry and chocolate chip, please."

Connor glanced at Lucy. "I'd advise extra napkins."

"I have three at home. I'm so outnumbered I know every trick."

"Bless you. I'd like the jalapenos and the potato skins with extra ranch, please."

"Good choice. You've been here a few times." She winked at him.

"I would like the fried chicken, please, with the mashed potatoes," Connor said.

"Y'all are hungry. We like that here. I'll be back soon." Lucy headed for the kitchen.

"Daddy... Is Uncle Rick going to feel it when the worms eat him?"

Early damn near snapped, but then he saw how there was a true fear in Jaxson's eyes. "Nope. He's not in there. That body can't feel a thing."

"Hey, guys, listen." Connor took Jaxson's hand. "The burial is for the people who love Uncle Rick? He can't feel anything; he doesn't know what's happening to his body, okay? Mother Nature will take it from here and return his body to the earth like it should be. It's totally fine; all of Uncle Rick's hurting is over. Okay? I promise."

Jaxson searched Connor's eyes, then glanced at him, so he nodded. Jaxson relaxed, then stared at his brother. "I told you. He isn't going to come and make me a zombie!"

Oh, for fuck's sake. "Seriously, Jay-Jay?"

"You know...braiiiiinsssss..." Jayden said in a goofy voice with his eyes crossed.

"I'm going to brain you. Don't terrorize your brother." Asshole child.

"Why not? It's my job!"

"Jayden." That was Connor's dad voice. "That's enough." Connor held Jayden's gaze until Jayden nodded.

"Yes, sir."

Lord help them, these two beasts would kill each other if they didn't love each other so much.

"I have waffles." Lucy set two plates down, and a stack of napkins, and put the syrup in front of him. "Just in case. Your food's up next, but I thought they might be hungry."

"You are an angel among women. Thank you." He helped Jaxson and let Connor deal with Jayden. Jaxson was messier, but less temperamental.

As soon as the boys' mouths were full, all the banter came to an end and the table got blissfully quiet. Lucy brought his food and Connor's.

"Okay, I'm ready for this."

"Hello, son." His dad stopped by the table. "It's done. Your Momma is hungry. A whole crew is following us here. You want us to take the boys when they're done eating? I'm sure she'd love to show them off."

"If you're up to it, sure." He needed to go to the ranch with Connor, talk to Demming. Breathe.

Jayden jammed a huge bite of waffle in his mouth. "Mm done!"

"Me too." Jaxson didn't even bother with another bite, he just got up and ran to his memaw.

"Sorry." Daddy shrugged sheepishly.

"For what? You're taking the hyped-up, syrupy beasts of doom." Early shot Momma a shit-eating grin, and she rolled her eyes at him, so dramatic that they all cracked up.

"They're not going to starve with me around for sure." Momma gave him a smile and a wink. "We'll keep them as long as you need."

"Sounds great, thank you, Momma." Connor adored his mother, and it showed in his husband's smile. "You're good to us."

"I love you all. My grandboys are my pride and joy."

Momma hugged Jaxson close. "How do you feel about some time at the park, and then some gooney golf?" She winked at Connor. "I promise no shenanigans."

"That's a pie crust promise, Momma."

Connor laughed. "You've already taken them to the barber, Momma. Oh—did you mean *their* shenanigans?"

"Daddy says tomorrow can be the train, Mamaw! The train!" Jayden bounced over, and one of the spoons went flying. Connor's hand shot out, and he caught it.

"Good catch, Dad."

"Thank you, Daddy."

They shared a soft laugh.

"You two eat." His dad gave them a wink and ushered the boys and Momma away.

Connor took a deep breath and let it out slowly. "Wow."

"Yeah. Yeah, I feel like I've been wrapped in a wet towel and beat." He had so much shit swirling around his brain, he couldn't stop it.

Connor nodded and sipped his coffee. "We eat, then we deal with...everything." Connor took a bite of his chicken.

Yeah. Everything.

There was a shitton of that. Early was sure of it.

6

By the time Demming was done explaining all the shit that needed to be decided on, dealt with, and provided for, Early's head was swimming.

He didn't know how he was going to deal with all this shit. There were the boys, Connor, the parents, Demming's imminent retirement, the ranch, the bills, the taxes...

Everything.

And Early couldn't decide if he was terrified or excited.

The boys were spending the night with their grandparents, and Early needed to either talk to Connor or get really drunk.

Possibly both.

As he approached the house, he found Connor sitting on the porch with a glass of wine. So, both it was, then.

"All done with Demming?"

"Yeah. That was intense. How's it going?" *I'm exhausted and worried, and I need a hug.*

"Oh, fine. It's barely five and I've opened the wine." Connor stood. He wasn't sure who moved first but he got his hug. "So, tell me."

"Demming wants to retire in October. There's a new set of mustangs coming to run the new BLM lease—don't ask me why they decided to go after new BLM land when Rick was dying. There are twenty pregnant heifers and six pregnant mares. I need to hire a new foreman, I need to deal with taxes and accounts and...god, Connor. What am I going to do?"

Connor gave him a tight squeeze, then let him go. "It's we, honey. It's always a we. What are *we* going to do? And for starters, I'm getting you a drink. You sit."

Early sat, and Connor came back with a glass of whiskey, filled slightly higher than was usually appropriate.

"Do you want the farm?"

"It's a ranch, love." He didn't know how to answer that, because of course he did. He loved raising his boys, but they were in school all day, and he loved Connor, but his husband was at work all day. Not to mention he loved this land, he loved cowboying, and he didn't know what to do.

"Really?" Connor sighed and looked right at him. "Fine. Do you want the *ranch*? And don't bullshit me. If you want it, we'll figure it out. But if you're feeling obligated, things are much easier."

"It—how could I not want it here?" How could anyone not love it here? "I'm going to try and commute down on the weekends maybe, see if I can hire someone..."

Connor shook his head. "That's ridiculous. I know how this has to go, at least short term, and so do you."

"So what about the boys? They've got another month of school? I'm going to have to be in Denver for that, one way or the other." If he spent the summer here, training a foreman with Demming, then he could be with Connor and the kids most of the school year, for sure. He'd just get his dad's help and figure it out.

"It's a month. I think I can keep us all alive at least that long. It makes more sense for you to stay." Connor picked up his wine and leaned back in his chair. "And who needs summer camp when you have a ranch?"

"What about you? What about your work?" *What about missing me? Needing me?*

"I don't know." Connor sighed. "That one is going to take time to figure out. I obviously can't—I don't know, Early."

"I don't know either. Maybe I'll come home Mondays and head out Thursday nights after the kids go to bed, until I can figure something out." Everyone could deal with shit for a few days a week, right? He couldn't just walk away from this place.

Connor shrugged. "That sounds exhausting. Maybe I should bring the kids out on the weekends?"

"Do you really want to spend eighteen hours a week in a car with the boys? Come on." Connor would rather eat raw tarantulas.

"Well, no, but is any of this about what we really want to do right now? This is about a short-term solution until we come up with the long-term plan, you know? You have a shit ton of issues to deal with here. Calves and mustangs don't care if it's Wednesday, and school is important too. So maybe we just... Zoom for a few weeks and suck it up. I can bring the kids down as soon as school is done. By then maybe we'll have the rest of it figured out."

Connor was too damn practical. He couldn't tell at all what his husband was feeling behind all that problem-solving.

"I—" Shit. "I'm not sure this is a great idea. The boys are going to drive you batshit crazy."

"Probably. Especially if Jaxson remembers he had a mouse before we left." Connor gave him an uncertain smile.

"What's really going to drive me crazy is sleeping without you. I don't remember the last time we did that."

"Me either. Maybe...maybe I ought to just put it on the market. Let it go." Just saying the words made him sick to his stomach and a little pissed off, that Rick put him in this position without planning.

"I promised you we wouldn't do that. You need to get this place stable and running, and then we can talk about the future. But with Demming and the taxes and everything... look. We're adults. We can handle a month apart. The kids will be busy, and I'll just make sure I'm around more, so they won't be without a parent."

"I'm not worried about that. You're a good dad." But he had to wonder how good of a father he was right now. He wanted to just...bring everyone out here and have them love the ranch like he did.

"We'll stay out the week, and then I'll rent a car to drive back to Denver."

Just that easy? How could it just be this easy? "Do you want me to drive you? Or hell, I have Rick's truck, but I can drive y'all."

"No, that's like a thirteen-hour round trip. Don't do that. We'll be fine."

He sat there and stared at his drink. He didn't know what to say, what to do. He was just about overwhelmed, and he just didn't know what to do next. So he sat and watched his drink throb with the beats of his heart.

Connor was quiet long enough to sip his wine and set it back down. "I keep thinking...you have inherited this amazing land, an amazing house, a place you've loved as long as you can remember and we're agonizing over what to do about it. How does that make sense?"

"I just—you have a whole life in Denver. I know that."

"I have a great life in Denver, but that life includes you."

"I sure as shit hope so." He stared at his husband, his heart pounding. "I don't want to fuck us up because I'm selfish."

Connor grabbed his hand and held on tight. "I feel the same way. Exactly the same. If I asked you to come home, look what you'd be giving up."

He just squeezed, telling himself to chill the fuck out. They inherited a multimillion-dollar ranch. It was just a month, and then they could plan.

This wasn't the end of the earth, dammit.

"I love you."

"I know. I know that with my whole heart. We can handle a little time apart while school finishes up, and then I'll take some summer vacation time and...there's an answer. We'll find it. We just need some time."

"I guess... I wish someone had given me some time, you know? Some notice so we could have planned." So he'd had warning.

"Me too. If we'd known even six months ago..." Connor eased up on his grip but didn't let him go. "There's nothing there but an argument that's not worth having."

"Well, at least we're on the same side of that argument, right?" He lifted Connor's hand up to his lips. "I love you, old man."

Connor slid over into his lap. "We're on the same side. Always. And who are you calling old, you geezer?"

"Have you checked your balls for gray hairs yet?" he teased, the chuckles starting. "I know I've been down there..."

"Uh-huh." Connor slapped his shoulder, but he was grinning. "I know why you like that hat so much; it covers up what's missing under there."

"Oh, don't even go there, you ass. I have plenty of hair." It was just short-short.

"Uh-huh. In certain places." Connor laughed.

He reached over and tickled Connor, playing with him, looking to make him laugh.

"Stop. Stop that. Goddammit, would you...ugh!" Connor gasped and squirmed in his lap and finally broke free, stumbling across the porch. He got a big, pink-faced grin. "Ha!"

"Ha?" He stood and started stalking his lover, trying not to think about all this mess.

Oh, Connor was so on board. His lover took slow steps backward until he bumped into a chair and gave Early a wide-eyed look. "Be nice, cowboy."

"I'll be nice, baby." They never got to do this. Be sexual in the open. He loved seducing his man. "I'm fixin' to be so nice."

"Mm." Connor licked his lips. "Not *too* nice, I hope."

"You ever fucked good and hard outside in a hot tub, Connor?"

Connor swallowed and slowly shook his head no, but a grin tugging at one corner of his lips told Early he was interested.

He grabbed the back of Connor's neck and tugged him in hard, kissing him fiercely. If they had to be separated, he wanted Connor to remember this.

Connor moaned and pressed against him, returning the kiss, fingers tugging on his belt loops.

He groaned and held on tight. He was going to grab lube and get the water heating. Then he was going to fuck Connor into next month.

Connor fumbled with his shirt buttons and nipped at his lips. "I'll get the—and you can—fuck, I want you."

"Uh-huh. Meet me in the hot tub. I need you. All of you. Now." He groaned and tore his shirt off as he headed to the Jacuzzi. It was quick and easy to start the heater and pull off the cover.

Thank god it was all clean and balanced.

Connor was breathing hard when he reappeared, barefoot and shirtless. "Got it. Oh, look at this thing. Wow."

"Uh-huh. It's cool, isn't it? We can bubble together, it's private, and it's all ours."

Connor set the lube down on a wide ledge and stepped in close and he could feel his lover's heat. "Mmm. Think of all the things we can do with alone and private. Better yet, show me." Connor kissed him, smoothing fingers like fire over his skin.

"Mmhmm. I'm going to make sure you don't forget tonight for days and days." He toed off his boots and pushed his jeans off.

"That sounds perfect." Connor shed his jeans too, and reached for him again, showing him how much he was wanted.

"It does." He loved the son of bitch so much, that it hurt.

The water was good and hot, and he loved the way he got to watch Connor climb in and head over to him. "Oh, this is nice." Connor waded a couple of steps, water lapping at his hips. "Decadent, right?"

"Yes." He reached out and gently pinched the tip of Connor's cock, looking to spark those sensitive nerves.

Connor hissed and caught his hand, tangling their fingers, and returned the gesture, rolling his nipple between wet fingers. "You are the sexiest man on earth. You still turn me on like the day I met you."

"Good." He wanted that and more, because he knew

what Connor liked now. He knew every hot spot and could play each and every one.

Connor chuckled, straddled his knees and sat. "So confident." Connor kissed him again, the connection hungry and needy.

He didn't feel it; Early felt desperate, but he'd be damned if he let it show. He wanted to make Connor sweat, remember that they were the real thing.

He grabbed Connor's ass, dragging their bodies together.

"All these handsome, strong cowboys out here are going to see is a hot rancher on his own. But you're mine, and they can't hold a candle to me. I'm going to make sure you don't forget that." Connor slid a hand under his sac and gave it a firm squeeze.

"I never would." No matter what. He would fight God Himself for his family.

"I know. But how about we make sure anyway?" Connor grinned at him and worked his prick slowly in a tight fist.

"Sounds like one hell of an idea. Seriously."

"Mhm. I think you should make my ride home just the right kind of uncomfortable."

"I intend to make you ache." He slicked his fingers and encouraged Connor to kneel tall.

"Please." Connor threaded fingers into his hair and shifted up onto his knees, spreading for him. "I'm yours."

All Early could do was get his lover ready for him, fingers stretching that tight, sweet hole. Connor rode his fingers, arching against him. "Yeah. I want that fat cock, cowboy."

"You ready?" Because he was aching, his prick heavy and throbbing. "'Cause I'm ready for you."

"Ready. Yes, I'm fucking ready." Connor practically growled at him and stretched up higher.

He pushed his cock back and used his other hand to guide himself to press into Connor, humping in just enough to make them both grunt.

"Oh god. Yes." Connor exhaled heavily, so Early leaned back, grabbed Connor's hips, and starting fucking his lover as hard as he could.

Connor's eyes popped open, then glazed right over as Connor grabbed at his shoulders and hung on. The water splashed around them as he dove into that tight heat, his husband doing what he could to meet him halfway, sending him deeper and deeper.

"Love." He bit out the word, his lips pulling away from his teeth.

"So much." He knew when he had Connor's full attention. The ranch could burn down around their ears right now and Connor wouldn't notice.

All he had to do was focus on his lover, give them both what they needed.

Connor rode him hard and squeezed tight around him. "So good. You feel...so good."

"Mmhmm..." He didn't have enough breath to say more. All his focus was on loving his man.

"Touch me," Connor begged, looking sweaty and a little wild. "Touch me. Make me shoot."

It took everything he had, to let go of Connor's hip and wrap his fingers around that fat cock.

"Yeah." Connor bore down hard, then rocked up, pushing through his fingers. So needy, his man. And not the least bit ashamed of it. "Oh, god."

"Shoot for me. Come on my cock, baby." Early stroked once more, good and hard.

"Yes, yes! Fuck!" Connor shouted and shot on cue, riding him all the way through it, muscles rippling, working him just right.

Early was right behind, holding on just long enough to send Connor flying before he clamped on to those hips and humped into his lover. Connor moaned, giving up everything for him to take, moaning with each thrust.

When he came, it was like he was flying into a million pieces.

"Yes, that's my man. So fucking hot." Connor kissed him, nipped at his chin, nuzzled into his neck. "Love you."

"God, I love you. So much." He wrapped his arms around Connor, holding on tight.

"I know. I do." Connor hugged him back, breathing with him, in and out, as real as they could be.

He nodded, telling himself this was ridiculous. It was a month. Not the end of the world. A month.

"We're okay, honey. We're lucky. You know we are." Connor settled in his lap, easing up on the hug.

"We are. I just feel...like I'm doing something wrong."

"Hey." Connor kissed him again. "If you're doing something wrong, then at least we're doing it together. Focus on what you need to do. I will too. And we'll keep talking. Every day, okay? We'll FaceTime you after dinner."

"Yeah." That weird sensation hit him again. What if they didn't need him?

"It'll be an adventure. The boys don't listen to me the way they do you. And I'm not half the cook you are either." Connor sighed. "I can do it though."

"And I'm going to work my ass off getting this place back on track. I swear to god." He was going to make this place shipshape.

"I would expect nothing less. That's what it needs. I know when we come back it'll be incredible."

"I'm going to have the bedroom painted for us, and replace the mattress, so it's ours."

Connor nodded. "That's a great room. I love the view."

"And a firm lock on the secret room door so the boys don't try bungee jumping?"

"God, yes." Connor's laugh sounded the most relaxed it had been in days. "They're not allowed in the hot tub either."

"No. I'll put in a pool." With a gate. A fence. Maybe an electric fence.

Connor's eyes lit up. "Right, I forgot you're rich now. You can just...put in a pool. Crazy."

"We, babe. *We.*" That was important.

"Sorry. We. Of course. I just never thought of myself as a rancher. This is...wild."

"Yeah. We'll figure it, right? You and me." Because the alternative wasn't reasonable.

Early needed his family.

7

"I can't find my other shoe." Jayden ran back up the stairs, taking them two at a time.

Connor sighed. Of all the challenges of the last two weeks, getting the boys out the door in the morning was the worst. "Come on, guys, you're going to miss the bus."

Jaxson turned in circles in the kitchen. "Did you make lunch, Dad?"

Oh, fuck. "No. I uh...you guys are going to buy lunch today." He dug out his wallet. How much was lunch anyway? Shit. "A treat."

"Yeah? Cool!"

"Cool." He stuffed ten dollars in each of their backpacks. "Don't lose it, okay?"

"Okay!"

"Found my shoe!"

Thank god. "Okay, out the door, guys. Look, the bus..."

"Run, Jayden!" Jaxson took off out the door.

"Bye!" Jayden went chasing after, only half-in one sneaker.

"Jesus Christ." Connor sighed as he watched the bus

drive away, then went to fill his travel mug with coffee and find his keys.

The first week without Early, Connor had felt like he totally had this. He'd left work early to meet the school bus, made dinner, given the boys baths, and read to them before bed. After everyone was tucked in, he'd pull out his laptop and get back to work.

The boys had mostly been good about it; they missed Early, but they'd managed ten or fifteen minutes of FaceTime every night after dinner while he was doing the dishes. He and Early hadn't really had time for a real conversation, their schedules were practically polar opposite, but they texted and sent pictures.

It wasn't *awful*.

But now he was at the end of week two, and he was exhausted. The boys had already started asking every day when they were going to see Early again. Connor had been staying up late working, then getting up early just to get five minutes of quiet. The boys had gone to a couple of after-school things this week—a band concert, the school play—and that had thrown off dinner enough that he'd ended up picking up pizza.

Twice.

The second time the kids reminded him that Daddy only ordered pizza on Fridays.

And he had two more weeks of this insanity.

His conversations with Early had been rough, too, and amounted to telling each other how tired they were, a quick, "I love you," and that was it.

Maybe he'd call from the car.

He wasn't sure what Early was doing—but he knew the list was insane. Early had to deal with probate, the ranch,

Demming. There were horses and cattle and feed and things that just didn't make sense.

He had a lot to learn. A lot.

He slid into his BMW and headed for work, then dialed Early as soon as he got on the road.

It rang a couple of times, then he heard Early laughing. "Hold on, babe! I've got a two-year-old on a lead, and she's *pissed!*"

"Goddamn, boss! She's fixin' to have your balls!"

"Shut up. It's okay, baby girl. You're okay. I got you."

How many times had he heard that comforting tone when the boys were little?

He shook his head. Early sounded happy. He missed that laugh. "Tell her I need those balls intact."

"Okay, y'all! Watch out!" Early was still laughing when he got back on. "Man, I forgot how hard that was. How are you, babe?"

"Having way less fun than you are, I'm on my commute. Just got the kids on the bus."

"Oh man. Yeah, I've been trying to work with this filly. She's been neglected something awful. I got her at the auction for twenty bucks. She needed a home."

"You bought a horse?" Wasn't Early busy enough already?

"Well, I bought twenty calves and saw the filly. You wouldn't believe her baby face. She needed a home."

"Listen to you, taking in strays." He wasn't going to pretend to understand adding work to everything Early already needed to do to get the ranch in order. "Have you hired everyone you need to help? Do you have a foreman yet?" What they needed was someone who could run the place when Early wasn't there. This single parenting thing wasn't something he wanted to do forever.

"I've hired a couple of hands and someone to deal with the house and landscape, but we haven't found the one that I can trust to run the place when Demming's gone." Early sighed softly, and then the sound of the wind stopped. "Yeah, please, man. Coffee sounds fine."

"I imagine it will take some time to find that right person. But you've got him until October." October felt like forever. He sipped his coffee, driving the long road toward Aurora. He didn't really know what else to say. This felt like a bigger conversation, one they weren't really ready to have yet. "Things are okay otherwise?"

"I miss you and the boys. My momma is always over here touching things. I have a sunburn."

"Ow. Sunscreen is a thing you know. We miss you too." Jesus, so much. But he didn't want to be a downer. "You missed the school play. I know it's your favorite thing." He poured the sarcasm on thick.

"Did you tape it? Can you email it to me?" Oh, Early sounded worried.

"There's a YouTube link, honey. I'll send it to you. You didn't miss much, I promise. Jayden wasn't even in it, and Jaxson had like one line."

"I am the man from down the road," Early intoned. "And I have no eggs."

"Give that man an Oscar!" He chuckled. "Stunning."

"I know, right? It's like I practiced that line for three months."

"Just like. Astounding. Anyway, he was brilliant of course." It was the worst play ever, but Connor was absurdly proud anyway. "I'll send the link when I get to work. I'm sorry I didn't think of it sooner."

"No worries. You've been busy as hell, I know. How are the boys doing? Okay?"

"They're good. School is fine. Jayden keeps losing his shoes every morning just as the bus is arriving, and I forgot to make lunches last night so I sent them with money." Wow. That got away from him. "They miss you."

"Put his shoes in his backpack. He pulls that one a lot. Jaxson will start hiding his underwear between the mattress and box springs next."

"Really?" Should he have known that? How did he not know that? "Why do they do that?"

"He believes, wrongly, that I won't make him go to school commando." Early's voice was smug. "I did slip a clean pair in his bag, just in case the seams on his jeans started to chafe."

He grinned. "You're so mean. I don't know if I can be that mean." He could be pretty ornery with opposing counsel, but he was usually kind to his clients. And his kids. "But I'll take it under advisement."

"Just be aware. The last thing you want is him rubbing his privates through his jeans all damn day. The teachers hate that."

"Good lord." He snorted. "I am now aware. You're an incredible dad, you know that?"

"I'm trying. I miss y'all. There's so much to show you. Hmm? No. No, I'll just take a sausage biscuit. Thanks."

"Is that Momma? Tell her hello for me." He'd like someone to make him breakfast. He was going to hit the drive-thru.

"He's one of my new hires. Ian. He's dealing with landscaping things, house stuff, handyman-type things."

"And breakfast. Handy. I've got two closings today, so I've got Mrs. Nolan on standby in case I run late, she even offered to make dinner." He knew he was going to run late. Not hours late, but too late to meet the bus.

"Oh, that rocks. I'll send her a text to say thank you. I wish I could make you supper."

"I do too. I miss our routine. I miss you." *I'm worried you're having fun on the ranch without me.*

"I miss you too. Nights are damn lonely out here."

He hadn't slept well since he'd gotten home. "The middle of the night is the worst."

"Yeah. I've been sleeping in the living room. Saving our room for us."

"Oh, honey. You can't sleep on the couch for a month. Save that amazing new mattress you're buying for us and go sleep where you're comfortable. I don't want you to wear yourself out." The couch? He understood though, sleeping in their bed was hard without Early in it, but he needed to be close to the kids.

"I just want to see you. It's been a long couple weeks."

Part of him was glad to hear that. "Should I drive the kids down this weekend? Or do you think that will just make the last couple of weeks of school harder?" He wasn't sure.

"I don't know. Do they have to go? What would they learn anyway?"

Surely Early was joking.

"Ha. Funny. It's school, Early. Of course they have to go." He had to work too; did Early think he was going to play hooky?

"Bummer. They're going to learn a ton out here. I have been running tests on the well water. It's in great shape. And there's a glorious bit of river toward the back of the property. Rainbow trout, honey. I'm getting fly rods for all of us."

"I'm sure the kids will love it. Hang on." He pulled up to the drive-thru and ordered an egg and cheese sandwich and another coffee. "Do you think we should come for the weekend or not?"

"Why don't I come out? I can be there Friday and stay through Monday, maybe?"

That would certainly be easier. "Can you do that? That would be great. We could surprise the boys."

"I don't see why not. I want to see y'all, and the next time I'll come and get you, and y'all can stay for a while, maybe?"

"We can definitely talk about that." The kids for sure. He still had a job, and he'd just taken a week off for the funeral. "I want to see you too. I feel like I'm missing an arm without you around."

"I hear that. I looked around though, and I don't have it. Your arm." Early's laughter was soft and utterly wicked.

"There's my dorky cowboy." He rolled his eyes. "I need two extra ones to deal with these boys, I'm telling you. They're going to be so excited to see you." He grabbed his breakfast and got back on the road. "I'm almost to the office, honey. Can we talk more later?"

"You know we can. I love you. Have the best day, yeah?"

"I love you. I can't wait to see you. Don't let that horse get your balls." He grinned.

"No, darlin'. Those are yours, one hundred percent. Just ask around."

He loved his man more than words. He was looking forward to hearing that darlin' in person again. "Damn right. You make sure everyone knows it." So what if he was the jealous type? "I gotta run. Be safe. Love you."

He hung up first because if he didn't, they might say goodbye for an hour.

Hell, if he wasn't careful, he'd be driving the kids to Durango after school this afternoon.

8

Early hadn't made it back to Denver, after all.

Momma and Daddy had wrecked the fuck out of their car, leaving Daddy with a broken rib, Momma with one arm in a sling. He'd had the vet out for a momma cow with an infected teat, one of the new hands had left along with five hundred dollars' worth of stuff from Demming's house and slit all four of his tires to boot.

His head pounded, and he closed his eyes for half a minute. Now Connor was coming with the boys, Connor was exhausted, and Early was going to explode.

It was dark by the time the BMW pulled in, kicking up dust, headlights bouncing as it rolled up the unpaved drive. He'd expected Jayden and Jaxson to be sound asleep in the back after the long trip, but as soon as the car stopped, the doors opened and the boys came tumbling out, voices cutting through the quiet night air.

"Daddy! Daddy!" They ran for the steps while Connor unfolded himself slowly from the front seat.

"Oh, my boys. I've missed you so much." He grabbed them both, his soul drinking them in like they were water on parched soil. "Lord have mercy, I've been aching for y'all."

"We missed you. Dad drove fast."

"We left school early and everything."

Connor came up the walk with a big duffel over his shoulder. The car chirped and the headlights flashed as he locked it. "I didn't drive that fast."

"I missed you." He met Connor's eyes, holding them. "Thank you for coming."

He'd needed them to come home.

Connor didn't even blink. "I had to. With everything going on? You need us."

"Daddy, I'm hungry."

"Yeah, they need a snack. We didn't stop for dinner." Connor saw him, heard him, but was focused on the boys. "A snack and then bed guys, okay?"

"I have stuff for turkey and bacon sandwiches ready, and I have some chocolate chip cookies. I made up y'all's bedrooms too." He went to grab some of the bags from the car.

"We have our own rooms?"

"Of course." This house was huge. Of course they did.

Connor caught his arm. "I'm going to the bathroom and then I'll unpack the boys' pajamas." He got a quick kiss. "Love you."

"I love you." He carried the bags upstairs. "Come pick your rooms, and then we'll make you some food, okay?"

"Daddy! We're out of school! I gotted an a hundred in art class!"

"And I won a ribbon for PE!"

"And I grew out of my shoes!"

"I brought my pillows and blanket!"

Early listened, letting the blessed chaos pour over him. Good. This was all good.

Connor disappeared for a bit while they picked rooms, and even though he looked tired, he was smiling when he joined them in the kitchen. "I can hear you hooligans from our bedroom," Connor joked, slipping an arm around his waist. "The bedroom looks incredible, honey."

"Thank you, darlin'. I wanted it to be perfect." He leaned over, whispering low. "The hot tub is ready."

That got him a warm smile and another, hotter kiss. "It's all perfect."

"Ugh. I told you they'd be all kissy." Jaxson rolled his eyes, and Jayden just chuckled, mouth full of sandwich.

"I haven't seen him in weeks, and I love him!" He covered Connor's face with smacking kisses.

"Eeeeew!"

"Daddy, gross!"

Connor laughed and shoved him playfully. "Wine, honey. Where's the wine?"

"Ooh... I have a surprise for you about that, but I have a bottle open." God, they were home. His man, his boys—this was heaven on earth.

"You have a wine surprise?"

He pulled a glass down and filled it, Connor watching his every move.

"I do. This house is filled with surprises, and I'm finding them all."

Jaxson pushed his plate away. "I'm full, Daddy."

"I'm ready to sleep in my bed, it's so big." Jayden looked pleased.

"Do y'all need showers?" He went to them, because he'd missed them bad as anything. "If not, go brush your teeth, and I'll come tuck you in."

"They're just going to get filthy in the morning. Just teeth is okay, guys. Everything is out on your beds."

"Okay!" They headed upstairs, no run left in them. His boys were tired now.

Connor sighed. "That was quite a trip."

"I'm sorry, darlin'. You know I wouldn't have missed last week, if things hadn't turned cattywhompus." The wreck had scared both his folks and him, if he was honest.

"You had to be here. I understand. Heck, if you'd been in Denver, I probably would have sent you here anyway. Momma's tough, but your dad probably was down for the count with that rib." Connor winked at him.

"Yeah. He is *grumpy*. Are you hungry? I have good bread and fancy cheese and mustard..."

"No. Thank you, but I am ready for a shower and to try out that big new mattress. You're good to me though." Connor's head tilted. "You are so tan. Even more than it looked on Zoom."

"I've been outside a lot." Instead of making his own sandwich, he snarfed up the boys' leftovers before cleaning up.

"I like it. You look good." Connor sipped his wine, those eyes never leaving him. "Really good."

"I missed you, too." Although he'd loved working too. This had been so big.

"We have a lot to catch up on. I feel like we haven't had a real conversation since the funeral." Connor finished his wine and washed his glass.

"We do." He walked right back up, begging a kiss. "I need you—not just your body. You."

"You." Connor kissed him easily, cupping his nape to keep him close.

His knees damn near buckled, and he leaned into it, trusting in the touch.

"We better tuck the kids in. Then you can show me around the new bed—I mean bedroom." Connor nipped his lower lip, then took his hand and led him out of the kitchen.

"And the hot tub. Did I mention the wine cellar?" He threw that one over his shoulder.

"The wine cellar." Connor snorted. "That's a good one."

"I hadn't seen it either. I'm leaving it for you to explore." It was cool. At least he thought he was. There was dust and spiders.

"Wait, you're serious? He kept wine too? This place is insane."

"Daddy tuck me in!"

"No, tuck me in first, Daddy!"

"Boys...you know how this goes. Get in bed." Connor rolled his eyes. "Just like normal."

"Yes." He winked at Connor, then pounced Jayden. "You were closer. Tomorrow Jaxson's first. I love you!"

Jayden rolled his eyes. "Silly."

"Yes, but I missed you. Bad."

"It's been forever. I didn't know a month was so long. Dad says he thinks we're staying for the summer though." Jayden yawned, sleepy eyes watching him. "That will be cool."

"I hope so. It was forever, and I need my boys. I have so much to show you tomorrow." And he wanted them to love it here too.

"I want to see the animals." Jayden yawned again and this time his eyes closed. "Night, Daddy."

"Night, son." He kissed Jayden's forehead, and then headed straight to Jaxson, finding him dozing. "Sleep well, son. I love you."

"Love you, Daddy. Biscuits tomorrow."

"He's half asleep, but his stomach is important." Connor chuckled from the doorway.

"Biscuits tomorrow, just for you." He tucked his little one in and then went to Connor. "And you, love."

"You have no idea how excited I am not to have to make breakfast tomorrow." Connor stepped back into the hallway. "Their rooms look great. You've been busy with this place."

"I'm trying. I wanted to make it ours, you know?" He took Connor's hand. "Yours and mine and theirs."

"I think that's what Rick would have wanted for you." Connor reached past him and shut off the hallway light.

"I hope so. Bed or hot tub?" Either way, he was touching to his heart's content.

"Oh, tonight? Bed. I'm beat, honey. It's been a long week." Connor stripped out of his shirt as soon as they went through the bedroom door. "Maybe a shower, though?"

"I can't wait to introduce you to the master bath." It made him feel like he was magical—rain bath in the shower, huge tub, fireplace. It was perfect.

Connor kicked off his shoes and slipped out of his jeans. "I got a quick peek when I came up earlier, but I didn't look around. I knew you'd want to show me. I can't wait."

"I do." He wanted Connor to be in love with this home, with the ranch. He wasn't sure he was ever going to be able to go back to being a suburbanite.

"You're joining me, aren't you?" Connor reached for him and untucked his shirt, then slid his hands up underneath it.

"Are you kidding? I wouldn't miss it." He flexed for Connor, knowing that his hard work was showing.

Connor grinned and started unbuttoning his shirt.

"Damn, cowboy. Let me see that." Connor pushed the shirt off his shoulders.

"See what?" What? He could beg for compliments. He wasn't a saint.

He turned, nice and slow.

"Mmm." Connor shook his head slowly. "Tan, muscle... you're even sexier than you were when I left. I didn't think that was possible." Connor took a hungry kiss, hands moving over his shoulders.

"Been working hard." He turned the overhead lights off with one hand, turned on the low blue lights in the next motion. "There's a fireplace too."

"Early..." Connor wandered slowly, taking it all in, eyes shining. "This is beautiful. It's so...romantic."

"And it's ours." He toed off his boots, his mouth dry at the sight of his lover, here. "All ours, darlin'."

"All ours." Something clouded Connor's eyes for a second but was gone just as fast. Connor tugged on his buckle and worked his belt open.

"I love you." He whispered the words against Connor's skin. "Fuck, I want to touch you everywhere."

"I've missed you so much. I hate that bed without you in it."

His jeans hit the floor and he stepped out of them as Connor turned on the shower.

"I need you more than sleep. More than anything."

"Yes. God yes." He dragged Connor into the shower, thankful as fuck for the tankless water heater.

Connor followed him in, the spray making his skin shine. "It's huge in here. Why in the world would we *ever* need a shower this big?" Connor's eyes were bright and happy.

"Mmm...fucking? Sucking? Stroking? Rubbing?" He

could go on and on. He reached out to get started on that rubbing, stroking Connor's heavy cock.

Connor hissed and braced a hand on his shoulder. "All of that sounds...feels good. Fuck, that is not the same with only my hand." Fingers found his chest, a wet thumb gliding over his nipple.

"No. No, this is love." And he wasn't too proud to say it.

"I hate being without you." Connor pulled him into a kiss, tongue shoving past his lips to tangle with his.

So stay. Stay here. I need you. He poured all his hopes into their kiss.

He could feel Connor everywhere—warm against his chest, hands moving over his skin. Their kiss went on and on, deep and hot, he swore Connor was trying to swallow his tonsils.

It was the easiest thing on earth, to stroke Connor's prick, roll the heavy balls.

Connor turned in his arms, making him shift his grip and pressed that tight ass up against him. They moved together, his prick sliding sweetly between slippery cheeks. "Love this fucking shower."

"Uh-huh. Magic." Connor was magical, pure love. He started rocking, his eyes rolling back in his head.

Connor braced his hands on the shower wall and pushed back giving him something to work against. "I'm going to keep you up all night."

"Promise?" Early bit Connor's shoulder, wanting to leave a mark.

"Yes." Connor groaned and went up on his toes. His cock jerked happily in Early' hand. "Fuck, I promise."

That was what he wanted to hear. Hell, it was what he needed to hear, if he was honest. He jacked Connor faster and harder, working himself against that sweet backside.

The tile and glass made Connor's harsh breaths even louder. "Early...fuck, I'm gonna come. I'm gonna..." He hardly needed the warning; he knew. They knew each other so well. Connor grunted and shot, and his lover's familiar scent filled his nostrils.

He grabbed Connor's hips, dragging them harder together. It was his turn, and he needed to come, to empty his balls.

"Yeah. Take what you need, cowboy. All of it." Connor's words were rough and breathless.

"Need you. Fuck, darlin'. I'm on fire." And it wasn't the hot water.

"Yeah?" Connor turned around and moved him back against the shower wall before slipping to his knees, where he was soaked by the rain showerhead. Water splashed over Connor's shoulders as that fucking clever tongue slid up the length of his cock and drove through his slit.

That was all he needed. Just that single, wild touch, and Early was shooting, his entire body bucking.

Connor looked up at him with glassy-eyed satisfaction as he striped Connor's chest, though the milky ribbons were washed away almost instantly by the shower.

"Fuck. Best. Shower. Ever." He sat on the shower seat and drew Connor up into his lap.

"It's incredible." Connor nuzzled his ear and kissed his neck. "Maybe I'll just move in here."

"Mmhmm...you would miss the new mattress then." And that would be a shame.

"I'll split my time then. Wherever you are, that's where I'll be." Connor's kiss was full of gentle love, the kind that lasts longer than a shower or a good night's sleep.

"Mmm...ditto." He got some shampoo and started

lathering up Connor's hair, fingertips digging in and massaging.

Connor leaned into his touch. "The boys are going to be up bright and early, they're so excited to be here."

"That's cool. You can sleep in. You've earned it."

Connor scrubbed him too and the smell of lovemaking was washed away, replaced by Irish Spring. "We'll see. I don't want to..." Connor shook his head. "You know, miss anything."

"I want to show you all of it. I want to make you breakfast and show you how the pool is coming and show you all the new horses."

"I can't wait." Connor shut the water off. "Honestly. I've been looking forward to it. And it's all the boys talked about the whole last week of school."

"I just thought about you and our boys. I want to sleep in our bed."

"Take me to bed, then." Connor handed him a towel, fingers grazing his cock as they moved away. "We'll snuggle a while, and then maybe I'll let you fuck me in our bed too."

"You do know how to make a man happy, darlin'." Balls to bones.

They left the towels in the bathroom and wandered toward their big, new bed hand in hand. "It's not hard to make you happy; we were meant for each other."

"Yes." He kissed Connor's hand. "House, turn the lights to twenty percent blue."

"House? What?" Connor turned in a circle as the lights dimmed and cast the room in a soft blue light. "Oh my god. Did you put that in?"

"Uh-huh. And the full-house music system. And the smart kitchen and vacuum."

"Okay. I bet the vacuum is fucking cool." Connor

grinned at him and climbed into bed. "Is this what ridiculously rich people do with their money?"

"This is what Rick started with his money, and that was before the crazy amount of insurance..."

Connor reached for him. "I don't even know what a smart kitchen is. Does it cook dinner for you?"

"Nope. But you can set the oven remotely and tell the fridge you need milk. It's weird as fuck." Early thought the music was great, but the kitchen? Dude.

"That's ridiculous. Does the fridge go shopping too? On that would be cool. Does it make an Instacart order? Do you even have Instacart out here in the boonies? Come here, you." Connor tugged him into bed.

"Uh-huh. But we got us a person. You give him a list. He has a business card." He pulled Connor in close. "I love you. I'm so glad you're here."

"I love you too. And I love this bed." Connor kissed him, then settled, resting against him.

It was a win, then. He got his family home.

9

Connor didn't sleep in. He was up with the sound of his boys and the smell of coffee coming from the kitchen. He hadn't slept much at all, in fact, because he'd kept his promise to Early. So he was a little sleepy, but otherwise felt better than he had in a month.

Except for the one thing he hadn't told Early last night.

But he had no intention of starting that discussion before coffee, so he finished brushing his teeth, dressed in jeans despite the heat and a T-shirt, and made his way to the kitchen.

"Dad!" Jaxson jumped up and hugged him.

"Daddy's cooking. It's all normal again." Jayden looked so happy.

It wasn't as normal as he wished it could be, but it was good for now. "Good morning, everyone. Hey you." He kissed Early's cheek and pulled a mug down from a cabinet.

"Good morning, gorgeous." Early patted his butt, the sausage sizzling in the pan, the scent of biscuits luscious. "How did you sleep?"

"Did we sleep?" He chuckled and poured himself some coffee. "I don't remember sleeping much."

"Mmm..." Early's grin was wicked, totally unashamed. "We can nap later."

"Works for me." He slid a hand over Early's ass as he walked by. "What's first on the agenda this morning?"

"Breakfast. Then a walk around the barns? The pool?"

"I want to see the animals." The boys said at the same time.

"Hey, Kitchen? Where are the plates?" He asked into the air in the center of the room, then laughed when there was no reply. "Smart kitchen, my butt."

"You turkey." Early rolled his eyes, all dramatic. "I was waiting for you to reorganize."

He opened and closed doors until he found plates for breakfast. "Ooh. I shared domestic chore. We must be married."

"The plates here are weird." Jayden snorted. "They're all colorful."

"Right? The boring plain plates at home are way more interesting." he teased.

"I like the plates—I want a purple one!" Jaxson raised one hand like he was in school. "Pur-ur-ur-urple!"

Jayden rolled his eyes. "Weird. I want the red one."

"Purple, red, I'll take this teal-colored one. And...yellow for you Daddy?" He set the plates on the table. "Who's hungry?"

"Meeee!" his boys sang happily. He loved seeing them smile.

"Yellow works. Who wants honey butter?"

"Me! Oh, Daddy! Me!" Jaxson almost turned over his chair.

"You know, nobody got excited about breakfast when I was cooking."

"All you make is waffles, Dad."

"Guilty." He smiled and shook his head. "I'm excited about being cooked for too. Can I have honey butter too, Daddy?"

"You can!" Early kissed his temple. "And I made breakfast sausage for all y'all. I'm thinking tacos for supper."

"TACOS!" The boys' scream split the air.

"Tacos." He nodded slowly. "Perfect."

Breakfast was delicious, of course, and he sipped his coffee and listened to the boys tell Early all about their grades and the end-of-school field day. When everyone was done, the boys ran upstairs to get boots and he helped Early clean up the kitchen.

Early was like a magnet, pulling him in. He didn't want to be more than a few inches away. "Thank you for breakfast."

"It was my pleasure, darlin'. I was missing our mornings."

He felt like he was keeping a secret, and he didn't want to wait much longer, but they could talk while the kids were playing with the chickens or something. "Me too."

"I have my galoosh...uh gal..."

"Galoshes, dummy."

"Jayden."

"Sorry," Jayden mumbled.

"Be patient, boys, and I'll take you to see the horses in a bit, fair?" Early winked at them, before asking him, "Do you want to come see too?"

"Of course. I want to see everything. Every little thing you're doing here." He needed to understand what made Early so happy here.

Early grabbed a ballcap and encouraged them outside. On the far side of the deck was the hole for the pool, then there was a lovely piece of lawn for the boys to play ball on.

"That's going to be a big pool, honey. Wow. They dug that in a month? How long before it's done do you think?"

"We'll be in the water by the end of next week, from what they think." Early squeezed his hand. "Do you like it?"

"Are you kidding, really? I love it." He tried to imagine the clear water and the boys doing cannonballs. He squeezed back, knowing damn well he wasn't going to be here next week to christen the pool. "I really do."

"Yeah? I tried to think about everything—exercise for you, fun for the boys, floating with a beer for me."

"You need one of those floating chair things with a cupholder and an umbrella." He laughed. "Hawaiian shirt, bright pink trunks..."

"Yes. I want matching shirts for us, though. I want to grill burgers and dogs and have beer in the cooler." Early sounded so happy.

"Daddy? This is going to be a pool? We're going to have a pool?" Jaxson sat hard in the grass.

"We are. We're going to have a pool."

"This is so cool. I am never going back to Denver. Everything here is cooler." Jaxson took off at a run toward the green lawn.

"Jaxson! I found a ball!" Jayden took off after him.

"Look at them go..." Early's expression was pure bliss. "Oh, darlin'. That's too cool."

He nodded. This wasn't getting any easier. "Honey." He slipped his arms around Early's waist. "I can't stay."

He felt Early deflate in his arms. "Why not?"

"Work." He sighed. He knew how Early felt, he didn't want to leave either. "I had hoped to get the week, but I have to be back for a meeting on Monday afternoon. I'm sorry."

Early nodded for him, eyes still on the boys. "I get it. I've got a bunch of balls in the air here too. The hooligans will be busy here, running their asses off and getting tan."

He watched Early carefully but couldn't catch his eye. "They'll have a great summer. Will you be okay with them here and everything else you're doing?"

"I will. This is a good place to be, Connor. This is a great place to grow up." Early sighed softly, chewing on his bottom lip. "I'm going to miss you. I was hoping you could stay."

"I want to. But I have a job, honey, and I... I can't do it here." He could quit. Early had plenty of money now, but he couldn't just walk out on his colleagues. "Plus, there's the house and all our things..." *I have a life and friends and... Starbucks.*

"Yeah. I hear you." Early frowned for a minute, and then the expression smoothed. "Do you want to stop by sometime today and see my folks? We can grab tacos on the way, if you want."

He'd fucked up. It was unavoidable, and that was why he'd waited until this morning to say anything. He'd selfishly wanted last night before they landed here. He sighed and let Early go. "Sure, sounds great." He stuck his hands in his pockets and looked away, watching their boys play. "How is your dad?"

"Sore. He'll be okay. They just need help. We can go into town around supper, so you can spend the day relaxing and hanging out, and we're not wasting time cooking or cleaning up." Early took a deep breath, then let it out. "What do the kids think is going to happen?"

"I haven't discussed it with them. I wanted to talk to you

first. Early." He reached for his husband again, taking him by the arm. "Even if I stayed the week, I'd still have to go back. I have a job." It was his turn to take a deep breath. "A job I'm going to quit, obviously. But they're friends too, so I can't just disappear."

"Hey!" That frown showed right back up. "I'm not asking you to just disappear. I wouldn't do that."

"I know. And I know I said I'd be here for a little while, but something came up. Don't shut down on me."

"I'm not. I'm disappointed. I miss you. I'm not being an asshole, I swear." Early shook his head. "I'm not riding your ass."

"I'm sorry." He put his arms around Early again. "I miss you too. I'm going to resign. Soon. I'll pack up the house, I'll get it on the market. Okay? A month just isn't enough time to completely change our lives around."

"I know you have a whole life there. I get it."

It didn't escape Connor that Early hadn't said "I have a life there" or "we do," but "you have a whole life."

He caught himself frowning this time. "You never said you were unhappy."

"I wasn't. I'm not. I just—this makes me feel...like I'm contributing again."

"Raising our boys is contributing." He shrugged and moved away once more. "I know you're happy here; it's in your eyes and your smile, it's...in your tan skin and all the work you've put into everything to make this house special for us. I know you did a lot of it for me, and I love it. I promise. I have no idea what I'm going to do here, but I'll figure it out." His husband didn't need him to contribute anything at all. Early was a zillionaire now, totally capable and in charge, and a much better cook.

Early blinked over at him like a confused owl. "You're a

lawyer, Connor. You practice law. You consult. You write a book. You write books about consulting."

He snorted, grinning. "I have zero interest in writing a book. But I appreciate the suggestion. Maybe I'll just be a kept man and sip piña coladas by the pool all day."

"Maybe you'll help me with the ten million bits about this whole fucking money part of this that I don't understand." And for the first time—there was a hint of a crack in Early.

He nodded. Money matters he understood. "Sure, maybe I can help. But you're a smart cookie, you'll get it eventually. Money has rules, that's all."

"I will. I'm sure I will." Early caught the ball in one hand, tossing it back into play.

"Good catch." He caught Early's gaze. "Hey. Look at this place. You've got this. We'll be okay. I love you."

"I love you too." Early winked at him. "You don't know how much."

"I have some idea. I'm a little sore this morning." He tossed a wink right back. "Very happily sore."

"If you're good, I'll let you soak in the hot tub tonight before you head home."

"Dad, let's meet the horses!" Jaxson came up and grabbed his hand. "This is the coolest place ever!"

"Let's do it." He held on to Jaxon's hand, but turned back to Early. "You promise, sugar daddy?"

Early didn't even hesitate. "I do. You have all of my promises, darlin'. Every one."

And he knew Early would keep them. Every single one.

"Ditto," he whispered as Jaxson dragged him off toward the barn.

10

One of the best parts about having the boys here at the ranch was that they ate their supper like they were starving, Early hosed their butts down, and they crashed in their beds.

Then in the morning, they got up and did it all over again.

The boys rode horses, learned to milk goats, swam in the pool. They played hours of football and tag and then they went to a kids' day out deal in town in the afternoon where they rafted and hiked and explored, before they came home to swim again.

Momma was sitting on the deck, finishing her glass of wine, while his dad tucked the boys in. "How's Connor doing?"

"Fine." He hoped, anyway. It was easier to be here with the boys because Early was working from six in the morning until nine at night. "He's really busy. Missing the kids, I think."

Momma gave him a sidelong look. "Really busy wrapping up his work there?"

God, he hoped so. "Yes, ma'am. It's hard, dealing with everything."

"What is he dealing with?" Momma sipped her wine. "Do you know?"

"Huh?" Early didn't follow, but he wasn't paying attention, either. He had to meet with the BLM guy tomorrow and head to the tax offices in town.

Ian came out with a fancy-assed chocolate cake, saving him, and he blinked. "Dessert, anyone?"

Early hadn't expected to hire a pastry chef wannabe for housekeeping and yard work, but it was cool as hell.

"My goodness, Ian. Cake for just the grownups?" Momma loved chocolate, though, and he knew she wouldn't say no. "Maybe just a small piece."

"This one is a little boozy, so the boys wouldn't like it." Ian winked at her. "Have a slice, and I hope you'll take the rest home with you."

"We'd love to, thank you." Momma took her piece, but Early shook his head.

"Oh, Early...you have to try a bite. I made you cardamom whipped cream to go with..."

Dammit.

"A little bit, then." He didn't need a ton.

"I thought he was more of a handyman?" Momma whispered, leaning over.

"I hired him to help with the yard and all, but he's been cooking when I don't have time. I think he needs a boyfriend to take care of." Someone young and hip and energetic.

"Hm." He knew that sound. That was Momma loudly not saying what was on her mind.

Ian handed Early his piece, looking fancy with a dollop of cream on top. "Enjoy."

"Thank you, man. I so appreciate it." He offered Ian a smile, not sure if he was supposed to ask Ian to join them. "Would you like to sit and have a piece yourself?"

Momma cleared her throat softly.

"Oh, no. I have dishes to do. But thank you, Early, you're so sweet. You'll both excuse me?" Ian took the rest of the food back to the kitchen.

Early leaned back and stared up at the stars. He wished Connor was here.

Momma patted his arm. "You miss him, I know. When do you expect him to move down?"

"He wants to pack up the house, deal with the firm, put things on the market..." Early figured the kids might be back in school before that happened. "I'll fly over to help him finish up, if y'all will watch the boys."

"Of course we will. We will always help when it comes to those boys, I hope you know that. They're little lights in our lives." Momma smiled at him.

"Little, filthy, sunburned lights." He loved it, though. These kids were covered in scabs and dirt and sweat.

"Just as kids should be. Just like you were. Covered in dirt and who knew what all the time. Pop put in that mudroom just for you."

"I know. I had the best childhood—here, with you and Pop and Uncle Rick. It was magic. I was so happy." It wasn't bullshit, either.

"I'm glad you're home, you know. I just hope Connor is ready for all of this. You spent a long while in his world."

That was his way of thinking. He'd been the stay-at-home dad. He'd gone to the city. He'd been suburban for their whole marriage.

It was time for him to have his dream.

Right?

"They're in bed. They're exhausted." Pop stepped out on the porch with them, cake in hand. "All this air is good for them."

"It is. They needed to be able to run amok some." He grinned at his dad. "I do like exhausted sons. A lot."

"Yes indeed. They don't complain much, do they?" Pop chuckled. "I'm feeling better. I'd like to come help some, just to be useful."

Momma's eyes narrowed. "You do, do you?"

"Yes. I have my grandsons and my son here. I want to hang out with them." Pop actually stuck his tongue out at her.

Momma snorted playfully. "You're a nosey old man, but it's true those boys like you."

"A little," Pop agreed, and they all laughed together, before his dad shot him a lot. "So, who's the baker?"

"He's the landscaper and a handyman."

Pop gave him a confused look. "No, I asked who the baker was."

"The handyman is also the baker. And he apparently makes dinner and helps with the boys too. Early thinks he needs a boyfriend."

"I do. Thank you, Momma." He rolled his eyes, but he had to grin. "And the boys love him."

Pop nodded. "I guess he's earning his keep. Is he staying here? It's awfully late to have help around."

"Yeah. He's staying in the bunkhouse. I—" He didn't feel comfortable having someone Connor never met sleeping in their house.

"Wise." Pop gave him a nod. "You ready, Mother?"

"I am." Momma set down her wine glass and stood. "I was so comfortable. It's such a beautiful night."

"It is. Y'all be careful going home. You want to take the

cake home for tomorrow? I won't eat it." He liked pie. Connor always got him cherry pie for his birthday.

"I'll get it." Pop went back inside.

"Give Connor our love, sweetheart. Tell him we're hoping he comes home soon." Momma kissed his cheek.

"Every day, Momma. I swear to God. Every day." And it hurt him, deep, having Connor away.

"I know." Momma gave his cheek a pat as Pop took her arm. "Goodnight, Early."

"Night, son." Pop gave a wave.

He sat and stared at the stars, just trying to recognize the different constellations he knew, which weren't many. When his phone rang it made him jump and wondered if maybe he'd dozed off. It could only be one person at this hour.

"Hey, darlin'. How's you?" He grabbed his beer bottle and stood, heading in to lock up.

Connor sighed. "Tired. It's good to hear your voice. How was dinner with Momma and Dad?"

"Good. Ian made this boozy cake. Momma loved it." He locked up and turned off the lights downstairs.

"Since when do landscapers bake cakes?" He heard a cork pop on a bottle of wine.

"I guess this one does? I sent it home with the folks. It wasn't my thing." He hadn't the foggiest idea. He guessed everyone had hidden talents.

"Weird. So, I packed up another room today. The downstairs is all done except the kitchen."

"Oh wow. Does it look strange?" He wanted to be there helping, but Connor said the boys were more harm in this case.

"It's...odd? Kind of sad. It makes it feel even more lonely here. But I keep telling myself it won't be forever."

"It won't. You say the word, and I'll come out, and we'll finish it up."

"I've got a ton of work this week, but I'll do the kids rooms next weekend and then I'll have a better idea of when I'll need you." Connor sighed. "I listed it today. The house."

"Yeah? Are you... Are you upset? Do you want to keep it?"

"There's no reason to keep it, but...aren't you going to miss it a little? It's our first house."

"Yes. We brought our boys home to that house. We taught them to ride bikes there. We have a thousand memories." But he wanted to make a million more.

"Yeah. Yes. And I know we have tons of time to make new ones, but... I don't know. I don't turn on a dime well, I guess. I'll get there."

"I know. This place is my home, so I'm drawn here." And he was going to fight to keep it, please Jesus.

"It is, I know. I just hate all this in between. This place is so empty. I need to get things wrapped up here and close this chapter."

God, he didn't want Connor to hate him, but the idea of going back to that house where he spent hours a day inside planning meals and looking for a job that allowed him to pick the boys up whenever they needed was enough to make him nuts.

Especially now.

"This is just hard for me, Early. I thought if we ever moved we'd discuss it, time it the way we needed to, I'd find a new job first...this just feels all backward to me."

"I didn't expect this either. I had no idea that Rick was planning this. None." And he knew this was weird—it was for him too—but dammit, he needed help with the ranch, with the moving parts, and Connor was acting like he couldn't do that.

"I'm venting to the wrong person, I know. I gave notice, honey. Three weeks. Just three more weeks, and I'll be on my way."

He almost offered to sell the ranch, to come back to Denver and go back to their old life, but he simply...couldn't. He wasn't meant to be cooped up in a perfectly normal house with manicured lawns and no dogs or horses or sheep.

His boys had chosen lambs of their own to show in the county fair next year. They were learning how to gather eggs, ride, swim for hours. Go fishing and raft. It was too good to walk away from.

"I know this is hard, darlin'. I appreciate that you're doing it."

Connor chuckled. "If I didn't know that, I wouldn't be. How are the boys?"

"Happy. Exhausted. I told them they had to wait for you to talk about getting their own dogs, which almost was a meltdown, but Jaxson held it together." Which was a huge victory, as far as he was concerned. "I told them they had to write a pro/con list to show you."

"Wow. That's creative. I can't wait to hear their lists. That will be fun. Not to worry, though, I like dogs. Puppies, I assume? What are you getting them?"

"I thought we'd figure that out when you got home. I need this to be our decision." Right, like he'd just get them puppies. Jesus.

"Oh, okay. Great. I just figured you'd know what was best, since it's your...thing. The animals."

His thing. The animals. Fuck, he wanted... Maybe he

needed to call a friend. Was Chayton in town? Any of the old crew? "Do you want to stay in Denver?"

At least he'd left all his old friends already. Connor hadn't even started.

"What?" Connor snapped. "How can you...why would you even ask me that?"

"Because I'm worried about you. Because you sound unhappy." *Because I've spent the last fifteen years making you happy, asshole, and I don't want to stop now.*

"Early. I'm here all alone, and I miss you and the boys. I know nothing about ranching, and I don't know what my future looks like. I just gave notice at a job that I..." Connor sighed. "Yes, I'm a little unhappy alone, and I'm a little terrified, but I'm ready to do this for you."

"I understand how that feels." And that was true. He hadn't known how to be a dad, he had never been able to use his degree for a single day, and he'd spent years swinging between exhausted and scared. He meant every word.

"I know, honey. So, I won't vent to you anymore, and you won't ask me if I want to stay in Denver again."

"You can vent. It sucks. This sucks being apart. It sucks having you there and not here. The boys miss you. I. Miss. You."

"Good. Keep missing me. And I'll keep missing you, and that will make all of this chaos worth it when I get there. I should let you go. I have an early start tomorrow."

"Me too. I'm taking the boys to spend the day with Momma so I can go to some meetings." And possibly have a beer with Chay. Just to relax.

"I hope they go well. I'll call tomorrow. I love you, cowboy."

"With all my heart, darlin'." He hung up, his heart heavy.

Was he doing the wrong thing?

Was he making a terrible mistake?

It was a bit late to be wondering that now.

11

Connor hit the gym after work. Hard. He'd needed to clear his head; he'd needed the endorphins and an attitude adjustment.

And it had worked.

He drove home with the windows down and the radio up loud, breathing in the Colorado summer air and looking forward to his call with his husband.

He had a plan. He'd made a list, and he was going to tell Early all the things he was looking forward to about moving to the ranch. He'd talked to his team, and they'd all agreed he should leave in two weeks instead of three. The realtor had people lined up to see the house this weekend.

It was a good day.

It was still a little early to call so he took a quick shower and had a sandwich for dinner, and when he was pretty sure the boys would be in bed, he scooped up his phone, grabbed his list, and sank into the couch to make the call.

"Hello?"

That wasn't Early's voice.

He put it on speaker and looked at his phone. It was

definitely Early's number and handsome picture. Shit. Had something happened? He suddenly felt sick. "This is Early's husband calling, who is this? Is he okay?"

"Oh, yeah. Hey. He's in the shower. He was stinky as hell over supper."

Over supper? "I'm sorry, *who* am I speaking with?" *And why are you answering my husband's cell phone?*

"I'm Ian. I watch the boys, cook for the family, do housework. Anything at all the boss needs to be happy."

To be what? Fucking *happy*? He didn't fight the flare of jealousy, but it was muted quickly by another horrible realization. "You're watching my boys? Wait... Ian the landscaper? The chocolate cake guy?"

"That's me. Chocolate cake every time Early asks for it."

The urge to snap, "my husband doesn't like chocolate cake," was huge.

He took a deep breath. "Listen to me, *Ian*." He didn't know what game this idiot was playing but he wasn't having it. "You are going to put my husband's phone down right now, and never answer it again. Am I clear? Just tell him... no, never mind. I'll call back. And you better not fucking be there."

He hung up fuming, and not even sure who he was more angry with—that smart-ass little twink or Early. The kids didn't need a nanny, or a cook, and early sure as shit didn't need to be made "happy" by anyone but him. He dropped his phone on the couch and paced the living room, trying to figure out his next move.

Call Early, obviously, but not yet. He needed that idiot to go home first.

Assuming he was going home...

"Stop it," he said out loud, just to make sure he heard himself. Early would never, ever cheat. Ever. He just wouldn't, any more than he would have an affair behind Early's back. Never going to happen.

But he knew what he had on his hands. Early was beautiful, kind, friendly...there was always going to be someone looking.

That didn't fucking matter. They could look, but there wasn't going to be any touching.

Or cooking.

Or watching.

Or—

His phone rang, Early's face popping up. "Hey, darlin'. How's it going? I was in the shower—I got into something in the yard, and you know how raw I get."

"I know. Ian answered your phone," he blurted out. Dammit. He'd wanted more time to cool off, to think about how to handle this conversation.

"What? No, that's not... Really? That's not cool." He could hear Early's frown in his voice.

"No. It's not cool, Early. And why didn't you tell me you'd actually hired a nanny, not a landscaper or a handyman or whatever? If you couldn't handle the kids, we should have talked about it." He was annoyed, and he didn't know how not to be right now.

"A what?" Early sounded like Connor was speaking Swahili. "I don't have a nanny. The boys go to that camp deal in the afternoons, and if I can't watch them, Momma and Pop have them. You know that. I don't need a fucking nanny. I can handle my boys."

"Well, Ian also says he looks after the boys and cooks for you all." He snorted. "Oh, and makes you *happy*—let's not forget that one." He couldn't help the sarcasm. Yes, he was jealous. So fucking what? That creep was in his house with his family and he was stuck in Denver. So, hell yes, he was jealous.

"What the fuck are you talking about? He watched the boys in the motherfucking swimming pool while I was putting a camera up so you could see them on your phone from anywhere!" Oh, now Early was yelling?

He blinked, Early's thoughtfulness making him forget his jealousy for a second. "You put up a camera for me?"

"Of course I did. I thought you'd like it now, and then even here in the house, you can keep an eye on them without leaving your office."

"You're the best husband ever. Thank you." He sighed. "But listen, you deal with that little shit Ian. Tell him he better back the fuck off, or I'm going to drive down there and cut off his balls. If he has any. I don't like his little game. Nobody gets to play house with you in our house but me."

"No. I want you. Here. With me. That's all I need right now. He's a kid, darlin'. I'm not in his market."

Wow. Was Early that clueless?

"I know, I'm not worried about you. But he wants in *your* market, Early. You follow me? He's staking a claim because I'm not there. He knew damn well who he was talking to. I introduced myself."

"Well then, he's a damn moron." Early sighed softly. "Lord, have mercy. Kids today. You have a good one?"

He quit pacing and poured himself a glass of wine. "Until Mr. Horny answered your cell phone, yes. It was a great day. I'm coming home a week early." The choice of the word "home" was deliberate. He was shifting his mindset. He was going to do better.

"Ooh... Yeah?" His FaceTime started ringing, Early doing the happy dance for him. "Woohoo! Home for pool parties!"

"Ha!" He laughed so hard he had to put his wine glass down. Oh, it was good to see that smiling face. "You're a loon." But he did a little happy dance for Early too.

"Oh, darlin'. I know I'm being a jackass, but I need you. You're—you're my best goddamn friend. This new life can't start until you're home."

"We'll have to go car shopping. I don't think the Beemer is the best choice for ranch life." He chuckled. "So I'll get a new car. And I'm going to be consulting some. And I want to learn to ride. I really do."

"You could get an Escalade. They're cushy and big enough for boys and friends and dogs and lambs..." Early winked at him.

"There will be no animals in my truck. That's what yours is for." He had to smile though. Boys and their friends sounded fun.

"You didn't even wince at the word lamb! I'm so proud." Early's grin was wide and...

"Are you naked?"

"Not totally."

His man, half naked with that so-called landscaper in the house? "Just shirtless, huh? Did Ian leave like I told him to?"

Early shrugged. "I'm in the bedroom. I haven't even looked. The boys are spending the night at the Harrisons— they have boys the same ages as ours."

"So you're home alone and half naked?" He grinned, feeling naughty. "You should be all naked."

"I want to be all naked. With you. Naked. Together." Early sat on the bed, and he smiled at the sight of the deep blue quilt. His favorite color.

"Well," he picked up his wine and headed upstairs. "We

could get close. We could be all naked together on FaceTime."

"We can. It's not the same, but it's better than jacking off thinking about you."

He set his wine down and slipped out of his T-shirt. "Of course it's better. It's jacking off to me jacking off. And I hit the gym today so I'm feeling pretty pumped up, I'll have you know." He'd never have Early's shoulders, or his tan, but he wasn't a slug.

"Uhn."

Oh. Oh, that was a pure needy sound, and it straightened his shoulders.

"Let's see." He propped his phone up against a pillow and stripped out of his sweatpants—slowly, for Early's benefit. His skin tingled at the idea of turning Early on, of knowing he was wanted. Early was never shy about that, and he'd be lying if he said he didn't love it.

Early licked his lips, eyes burning into him. "Damn, darlin'... I can damn near smell you."

He loved the tension in his husband's voice. He knew that sound so well. "I just showered, so I smell like soap and shampoo. Take your jeans off, cowboy."

"Damn, this shower needs you in it. I need to be in you." Early's zipper made the best sound.

"Two weeks, honey. Two, instead of three." He leaned against the headboard and arranged the phone just so— Early would get a decent view. He touched himself—it wasn't the first time Early had watched him jack off, hell at this point in their marriage, they'd done just about everything, so he wasn't self-conscious at all.

"Fourteen days. God. Fourteen days and you'll be in my arms." Early crawled up into the bed.

"For good. Fourteen days until the hand around my cock is yours again. Until I get to keep you up all night and feel you all day long." He moaned, that thought bringing more heat to his fingers. It climbed up his chest too, arousal making him warm.

"It's too long, but it's a goal. Fourteen days. I'm going to tear your ass up." Early's eyes were eating him alive.

"I'm going to let you, and I'm going to love it." His own need was building so he got a nice firm grip and stroked himself like he would if he were alone, only his eyes were on Early instead of closed and imagining he wasn't by himself. He slid one hand over his abs and higher up to pinch and roll a hard little nipple between his fingers, the little burn making him hiss.

"Damn, you're pretty." Early began to pant, tongue flicking out and wetting his lips.

"All yours, cowboy. Every inch." Jesus, the wasn't going to last too much longer, not with Early making love to him with that look. "You're going to make me shoot, honey."

"I can handle that. I wish I was there. I would lick you clean."

"I wish..." He took a shaky breath and puffed it out. He didn't want to pop off like a fucking teenager, he wanted to bring Early along with him. But it was a fight. "Fuck, Early."

"Mmm...we haven't done that in a long time." Early was trying to kill him.

He shouldn't be surprised; Early had always had more patience than he did. More control. It was maddening. And hot as fuck.

"You want it, huh? Okay..." Early wanted a show, he was on fire, and he was so close he didn't even want to hold off anymore, so he'd give Early what he needed. He worked his cock with practiced strokes and sweeps across the head. "Okay. Fuck... Early..."

"Love you, darlin'. So hot. Shoot for me." Early's voice was a deep growl.

"Yes." Yes fucking please. Two more swift, light strokes and he went right over the cliff as if Early had pushed him, gulping air and shooting ribbons over his belly, soaking his fingers.

"Jesus..." Early watched him through the aftershocks. "Pretty son of a bitch."

"Now you. You, honey. Let me see you." He was flying, but he wasn't going to relax unless he knew Early was with him.

Early nodded and started tugging off, moving with long, slow, measured movements guaranteed to drive him crazy.

He missed Early so much. Not just like this, but this too. "You're all my eyes can see, you know that? You're my everything. I want to touch you so badly."

"Soon. Soon, darlin'. We're going to have so much fun together." Early's teeth sank into his bottom lip.

"In the hot tub, the shower, our big new bed, and if your parents take the kids for the weekend, the possibilities are endless."

"Mmm... I bet they so would..." Early's breath deepened, and the color rose in his cheeks. "Soon."

His husband was beautiful. It was crystal clear to him now, as he watched Early bring himself off. Denver didn't matter, the house, even his job didn't matter. What mattered was Early. He needed to be anywhere Early was. "I love you."

"More than life." Early bit the words out and shot, arching as he did. It would have been perfect, if they'd been together.

"Fuck." Connor swallowed hard, still catching his

breath. Or maybe Early had just stolen it again. "We deserve better than this, but this was fucking nice too."

"It didn't suck." Early winked at him, and that smile was jubilant.

"I think maybe I'll sleep better tonight. Maybe." He certainly wasn't worried about the handy asshole anymore.

"I miss you, but it's better, knowing there's a date. A moving van. A time I'll have you in my arms where you belong."

"Will you come up to close up the house with me? We could drive home together."

"Yes. I'll fly in next week. We can have a week together. You. Me. Closing this part of our life up." The immediate answer suited him completely.

He knew Early wouldn't say it if he couldn't swing it, but he had to be sure. "The whole week? Are you sure you can do that? The kids will be okay? The ranch?"

"I'll make sure with my folks. And Demming will be here for another few weeks, so yes. It better be."

"Okay. Okay, great. So one week then. I'll see you in a week." He might not sleep after all, he was so excited. "A week."

"Yeah. I'll get a plane ticket in the morning. I love you."

"I love you. Text me your plans. Kiss the boys for me." He smiled at the handsome face on his phone. "Goodnight, honey."

"Good night, darlin'. I'll call you in the morning." Early touched his phone like he was stroking Connor's face.

He blew a kiss and hung up. Hanging up was the worst sometimes. But his good mood was back. And his man would be here in a week.

Life was good. Strange, different, but good.

12

Early had kissed the kids goodbye at five a.m. and grabbed a little puddle jumper to Denver. He was going to have to hit the ground running, which was fine, because he was going to have to convince his husband to leave a day early or drive overnight.

The boys' summer camp was having a family day, and Early wanted Connor to be there. Connor deserved to see all they'd been up to.

He hustled out of the tram, heading out past baggage, texting Connor with his location. It was so busy, so loud, and it felt so weird, already.

meet you there

Connor texted back right away, and as he stepped out to the curb, he could see the BMW headed his way. He waved, and Connor double-parked and popped the trunk.

Early tossed his bag in the trunk and hopped in the car. "Hey, you."

Connor looked tired, but he was smiling. "Hey." Connor

leaned over and took a quick kiss, then drove off, dodging pedestrians and taxi cabs. "Was your flight okay? You got up early."

"It was fine. Have you eaten? Do you want breakfast?" He reached out to touch, because he had to. "I missed you."

Connor dropped his hand from the wheel for a second to cover his. "I don't want to have to say that again for a long, long time. Maybe never. Never would be okay."

"Fair enough." He brought Connor's hand up to his lips, kissing it gently.

"You're not going to believe the house. It's in boxes, even the kids' rooms...it's been awful to be here with all of that by myself. I'm...just really relieved you came."

"Of course. I wanted... I want to help finish this with you, darlin'." Connor deserved help, support, and a lot of loving. Early was going to make this okay for his lover, if it killed him.

"I just...we need to figure out what furniture we're bringing and donate the rest. The kitchen is going to be a bear, and I haven't even looked at the basement." Connor glanced at him. "And I have to work a couple of days this week. But I've cleaned out my office. I just have to bring the boxes home."

"Fair enough. I want to try and get us home Friday for parent's day at camp. I didn't tell the boys we'd make it, but I'd like to."

"Oh. Friday? Hm. Okay, we'll do it. I want to go, I've missed everything." Connor sighed.

"No. Just summer camp. They start 4H soon, there's kayak lessons, and pottery lessons."

"Pottery?"

Early shrugged. How the hell did he know? "Momma

took them to some art class. Now they want to make pots with her."

"Well, I feel like I've missed everything. They look so big." The congestion didn't get better until they were well away from the airport, but Connor seemed to relax a little as the road opened up. "Are you hungry?"

"I totally can be, but we can order some doughnuts at the house too." He was easy. He had Connor. Life was good.

"Let's grab some egg wraps to go and head back to the house. We need to make a plan if we're going to get home by Friday morning." He could see the wheels turning as Connor thought about what needed to be done. "Hopefully we can reschedule the truck. I'll let you call; you sweet talk better than I do."

"I bet we can. I'm irresistible; just ask you..."

Connor laughed, the happy sound filling the car. "Utterly. I've seen your cannonballs on the pool cam. Who could resist that guy?"

That pool cam had been a stroke of genius. "No one, thank you. Can you believe how fast Jaxson can move across that pool?"

"Right? He loves it. Maybe his school will have a swim team."

"They do. Swim team, hockey, football, wrestling." It wasn't Denver, but it didn't suck. "They've already met the 4H leaders, and they like them."

"4H." Connor nodded. "It's hard not to feel like you've all started something without me. But I'll catch up."

Oh, poor guy. It wouldn't take long. These kids were ready to be a part of everything, and since everyone knew his folks, and a lot of them knew him, it was easy. "None of the insane, oh my god school shit has started. 4H is year round. Lambs. They have lambs."

"I know exactly nothing about lambs." Connor chuckled. "But I guess I'm going to learn, huh?"

"Yeah, they loved the stories about shearing. Jaxson has a black one, and Jayden's is white."

"How are you, honey?" Connor's tone softened in that way it did when something was important, when he was really listening. "I mean with everything? How are you managing?"

"It's harder than I thought it would be, but it's satisfying too. Things are growing and thriving, and it's fascinating, you know?"

"And you can see doing this forever? I'm not being cynical, I'm actually interested."

"I can—we're raising cattle for meat, sheep for meat and wool. There are wild mustangs on the BLM land, draft horses and two well-bred Thoroughbreds. We have chickens, ducks, and we're converting three acres to farmland." There was a good chance that they could be self-sustaining in a couple of years.

"Wow." Connor looked thoughtful as they pulled off the highway. "That's amazing. And are you still looking for a replacement for Demming, or...?"

"I think we need someone." He could manage on his own, but he needed time to be with Connor, the boys, and he needed a manager. "It's just about finding the right person."

Connor laid a hand on his arm and squeezed gently. "Is it awful of me to admit that I'm glad to hear you say that?"

"No. No, I want—I mean, what good is this opportunity if I miss time with you and our boys?" He wanted to be able to enjoy all this—together.

"That's how I feel. We should have more time together

now, I think. I'm going to work, but on my terms because...
well, I don't really need to do I?"

"Not for the money, but for the love of it, right? And
we're about to have two incredibly busy young men to deal
with." Those two wanted to try everything. Everything.

"I'm in. I'm so in." Connor pulled into the driveway and
parked right out front. "No room in the garage."

From the outside, the house looked exactly the same, no
sign that they were moving at all. But walking through the
front door, everything changed. There were only two boxes
in the foyer, but there were stacks in the dining room and
living room. "Welcome home."

"Home is in Durango. This is our old house." And he
was ready to put his head down and get to work. "Alexa, play
karaoke music!"

"Old house. Right. Home is where our kids are." Connor
leaned close to his ear. "Home is where you are." Connor
pinched his butt and danced off to the kitchen.

That was right. Home was where they were. Together.

With all their shit.

13

"I can't believe this is your last day."

Connor had heard that several times this morning as his colleagues dropped by his office—his former office—to say goodbye. They'd had a fancy breakfast together complete with a champagne toast to send him off, and he had a box full of going away trinkets that he'd been given too.

These people were coworkers, but a lot of them were friends too, and he'd miss them. "Thanks, Jackie." A text came in from Early, the third or fourth random question about the basement, and he answered it. "Sorry, I have so much going on." He gave her a hug. "Really, thank you. I'm going to miss everyone."

"Keep in touch?"

"You know I will." Would he? Or was that just a thing people said to make an awkward situation seem less of a big deal? He didn't know.

"Honestly. I mean, if you start your own practice, virtual work is a thing!"

"You know it." He wasn't sure about starting a full

practice on his own, but at this point he wasn't ruling anything out. He led Jackie to his office door. He needed to finish packing up. "I'll let everyone know when I'm settled in."

"Do that. Safe travels, Connor."

He managed to escape her and closed his door slightly to deter people, then went back to loading up his box. He only needed one; everything about work had to stay with the firm, including his laptop. But he had plenty of family pictures and a few awards, his personal files, and the leather desk set that Early had gifted him for his desk when he started with the firm.

Memories. That's what he was taking home with him. Lots of memories.

His phone rang, and he was surprised to see it was Early's Mom. That couldn't be good. "Momma? Everything okay?"

"Oh, fine. Early says it's your last day, so I was just calling to say we can't wait to have you here with us, finally."

Finally. She was very sweet and meant well, though. "Subtle as always, Momma. I am packing up, and I am looking forward to see you all too."

"I'm sure you miss your boys."

"I do, very much." *And if people keep interrupting me, I'll never get out of here.*

"Early missed you terribly, you know."

"I know, Momma. I missed him more."

Momma chuckled. "I'm not sure that's possible."

"Hey, Momma, I have to get things wrapped up here, we have a drive tonight."

"Oh, of course, don't let me keep you. See you tomorrow at family day?"

"I can't wait. Honestly." He was impatient to get home now.

"Good. Bye now."

"Bye, Momma." He hung up and opened up his laptop. Just one more email and then he could turn this in and get moving.

"Hey, Connor?" There was a light knock on the door.

Jesus Christ. "Hey, Kit, come on in."

"Hey. Wow. I can't believe—"

"It's really my last day. It is. It's crazy right?"

Kit smiled, embarrassed. "So...about the Lunar deal."

"I sent you an email with the status, and everything you need is in the file I left on your desk." Kit was nervous about him leaving, he knew. "You're going to be fine."

"Yeah, you're only a phone call away, right? I can't believe you're moving to the middle of nowhere on a ranch."

"It's not the middle of nowhere, it's just a big property." A huge property. Which, okay, did kind of made it the middle of nowhere. He looked around his office. "I think I have everything."

"Are you sure?"

Was the question "are you sure you have everything" or "are you sure about leaving"?

The answer was the same either way. "Yeah, Kit. I'm sure." He put the lid on his box and picked it up. It was time to go before someone else stopped him. "I'll be in touch. I want to do some freelance. I'll probably call next week."

"Okay. Well, enjoy your new adventure, huh? I mean, a ranch! Cool."

His phone buzzed. He put the box down and pulled his phone out, afraid of what it could be this time.

Hey. Love you. Moving truck is gone. Woo!

Oh, thank goodness. Some good news. "Sorry, Kit... It's Early."

> I'm just trying to get out the door. Be there soon.

He lifted his box again. "Gotta run, Kit. You've got this. Take care." He didn't wait for Kit to answer, he just made a beeline for the elevator.

Early was waiting for him at the house, and his boys were waiting for him in Durango. The pool, the amazing shower, the hot tub—those were all waiting.

The drive back to the house was both too long and too short. He was ready to see Early, but he wasn't as ready as he thought to see the house so empty. "Wow." He stood in the foyer with Early, an arm around his husband's waist.

"Right? It's insane. I sort of want to load the Beemer in a hurry and go, because it's so weird." Early held on tight.

It was weird. And it didn't feel like the place he wanted to remember now that it was empty. "Yeah. Yeah, let's just do it. You want to? We can get dinner on the road."

"I'd love that. There's not a lot—the coolers, the food, the suitcases, our pillows, and the picture of the four of us that goes above the mantle." Early insisted that the portrait needed to travel with them.

He hadn't argued, it was possibly their most important possession. It represented the day they became a family. "Everything in the trunk except the portrait. That can go in the backseat. I left a blanket out for it."

The car ended up way more packed than he'd intended, but there was room to see and for both of them to fit in.

Early looked over at him, face serious. "Are you ready for this, darlin'?"

"I don't know. Are we ever really ready for anything, you

and I? Were we ready to get married? Ready to adopt the boys? How did we know? I think we just make the best decisions we can and jump in with both feet." He trusted in what he and Early were together and that was that.

"So long as I have you beside me, that's what I need. Let's go home before Momma drowns the boys in the river."

He laughed and gave Early a sidelong look as he started the car. "She called me, you know."

"Oh god. She is panicking that we're going to decide all of the sudden to fly to Belize and leave her with the boys."

"I don't think so. I think she was making sure I wasn't getting cold feet." He was pretty certain that was it. "She wanted me to know how much you'd missed me."

"I did." Just soft and simple, no bullshit. "I'm not happy without you. We're a family."

He nodded, turning out of the driveway for the last time. "I told her I missed you more."

"This time, I bet you're right. I had the boys to keep me busy, and I wasn't trying to pack a house." Early turned to face him. "Tell me one thing you're excited about."

"One thing? I can't even pick just one." He'd focused on his list to get him through packing the kids' rooms. "Seeing the boys. The pool. Being self-employed. Learning to ride. Buying a truck. Finding a hat that suits me. You want more?"

"Absolutely. I want everything." Early's smile was bright as the sun.

"Um. Seeing the mustangs out the kitchen window. Our shower. The first day of school. Not having to drive to work in the snow. Setting up my home office. Making love in our amazing bed. Dogs."

"Oh, my god. I didn't tell you. They have a whole pro-dog presentation for you. It's hilarious." Early's laughter tickled him. "They want a puppy apiece, plus a little foo-foo dog for you."

"That's amazing." He laughed along. "They think I want a foo-foo dog? I want a big dog with a big bark for that big house." Really, he didn't need a dog at all, but if he had to...

"They chose a picture of a toy poodle with pink toenails. I didn't even get a dog. I think you need a Saint Bernard."

"We. Not me, *we*. You want a Saint Bernard? Maybe we should let the boys get theirs past the puppy stage before we add to the pack." This drive was going to fly by. He and Early knew how to talk when they wanted to.

"God, yes. Puppies are rough. Those boys are going to have to work hard at this." He shook his head. "They hit their beds exhausted now."

"I guess that's good. Work hard, play hard. I really can't wait to see them. Hug them. I'll even be nice about the pink toenails on my poodle."

"They miss you too. I told them we'd be back Saturday, so they're going to be over the moon tomorrow for family day."

"Oh, it's a surprise? That's great. I love that." It was so worth getting everything done a day early. "I'm even more excited now."

Early nodded. "This way, if we couldn't, they weren't disappointed, you know?"

"You must be a parent." He gave Early's knee a squeeze before putting both hands back on the wheel and turning onto the highway. "We're going home, honey."

"Yes, sir. Let's do this. I'm so ready."

They headed west, leaving the sun to chase them.

14

They'd gotten in long after the boys had been in bed, but Momma was up, waiting for them, just like she'd always had, smiling and hugging them both, needing her family home before she crawled into the guest room with Pop.

They'd showered and crashed, curled together in their big bed, holding each other like they were afraid they'd lose each other in the night.

When the sound of thundering feet sounded on the stairs, they were still snuggling in under the heavy comforter. Someone—someones—had seen the car. Early glanced at his husband, who was pretending to still be asleep.

"They're coming for you."

Connor's lips curled in a smile. "I know."

There was no pretense of a knock, the bedroom door just burst open, and Connor pulled the comforter over his head, pretending to hide.

"Dad! Dad!" The boys jumped on the bed, climbed over them, and tugged at Connor's pillows. "Dad!"

Connor threw the comforter off and grabbed them both, pulling them into a big group hug. "My boys. Oh, I missed your faces."

"We missed you!"

"We wanted you to come home so bad!"

"We love you!"

"Can you come to family day?"

"Can you tuck me in tonight?"

"No, me!"

"No! Me!"

"Hey, hey. The answer is yes to all of it, but calm down, guys. One thing at a time."

He gave Jayden a wink, and Jayden nodded and took a big, deep breath. Jaxson watched his brother and then did the same. He loved how excited they were though; he knew how much that would mean to Connor.

"Oh, very good, Jayden. Thank you." Connor ruffled Jayden's hair. "So. I am coming to family day, and I will tuck you each in tonight. I promise."

"Dad is home—like home-home, for good. The moving truck is coming tomorrow." He leaned back, soaking in the sight of his family right here where they belonged.

"Mamaw is making breakfast. You have to come sit next to me." Jayden slid off the bed.

"And me. Come on, Dad."

Connor scootched toward the edge of the bed and scooped Jaxson up. "Okay. I can do that. I will be downstairs in two minutes."

"Cool. Mamaw says there's coffee and French toast and bacon, so yay."

"Rock on. I'll go down and help." He kissed Connor's cheek. "Good morning, darlin'."

"Don't you go anywhere yet." Connor caught him and

gave him a real kiss, one that had the boys making disgusted noises as they left the room. "Good morning."

"Mmm...good morning." Connor was home. Really home. "I slept so good last night."

"Like a rock. Although, we got in so late that I'm going to need coffee to keep up with the boys today. Stat." Connor's smile wasn't tired though; it was keeping up just fine.

"I have no doubt there's coffee waiting for us. None at all." In fact, he could smell it, the bitter richness floating up the stairs.

"Just going to brush my teeth." Connor got to his feet. "I still love our bed. Ooh...and I still love, love, love this bathroom."

"And we have a secret room. A dressing room. A swimming pool."

"We are so spoiled." They freshened up at their side-by-side sinks, grinning and being goofy with each other in the bathroom mirror. Connor took his hand as they went downstairs, holding on a little tighter than usual. "Mm. I smell the coffee."

"You do. And French toast and bacon." Momma smiled at them. "The boys are out in the pool already. They ate."

"So much for wanting to sit next to me." Connor rolled his eyes, but kissed Momma on the cheek before pulling mugs down. "Thanks for cooking. And for coffee. What time does this family day thing start?"

"One p.m. at the park. Bring sunscreen. You're in charge of juice boxes and cut up fruit for fifty."

Connor's eyes went wide, and he looked between him and Momma. "Wait. Did you say for *fifty*?"

"Yep." She dished up their breakfast. "I'm heading home, boys. I'll be there later!"

Connor just gave a half-hearted wave as Momma

practically ran out the door, then sat with his French toast. "Well shit. We better go shopping. Did you know about this?"

"I figured we'd have to buy something. We'll stop at City Market. No big."

"Cut-up fruit for fifty is kind of a *big*, honey." He got a grin. "Juice boxes are heavy too. I can't wait to watch you carry them."

"We'll take the truck and the big wagon. It'll be perfect. I will call the grocery store though and warn them." Ten of the big packs ought to work, right? Right.

"Okay." Connor sighed dramatically. "But carry at least one to show off for me? I really want to see those biceps at work."

"You mean these?" Early flexed, pecs tensing.

"Hell, yeah." That drew Connor right to him, fingers sliding over his chest. "Damn, honey."

"It's been good for my dad bod, having physical work to do."

"I'm not complaining." Connor kissed one flexed bicep before he relaxed, then sat back down to eat. "I wonder if I'll tan? That would be cool. I hope so, I don't want to spend what little is left of the summer bathing in sunscreen."

Connor would, though. It would take a while for that pale, nine-to-five skin to get used to being out in the sun more often.

"There's a shade we can pull out if you need to. First, breakfast. Here or out on the deck with the boys?"

"Let's go watch the boys from the deck while we eat. But no shade, I'm going try to tan, dammit." Connor scooped up his plate in one hand and his coffee in the other.

Early followed along, laughing as the immediate "Dad! Watch me! Dad! Dad! Lookit!" started.

"I'm watching!" Connor did watch, eyes on the boys as he sipped his coffee, his breakfast forgotten. "Hey, nice dive, Jayden!"

"I can swim all the way across, Dad." Jaxson pushed off the side and swam.

"You're a fish, Jax." Connor was all smiles. "This is amazing."

"They sleep like the dead, darlin'."

"Have you registered them for school, or is that my first job on the ranch?" Connor winked at him.

"I thought we ought to do that together. I want the community to get to know you. I went to school with the principal of the elementary the boys will go to, for chrissake." Early's grin was sheepish. "In fact, she was the first girl I ever kissed."

"Oh, I cannot *wait* to meet her. How old were you?" Connor finally remembered his French toast and dug in. "We can compare notes."

"Fourteen. It was spin the bottle at a party. I thought I'd die." Early chuckled. Man, he'd been so confused, so worried about what he was—or wasn't—feeling, so friggin' at sea it wasn't funny.

"Aww. Man, if I'd been at that party..." Connor chuckled. "I knew exactly what was up by fourteen. I'd have been praying that bottle landed on me."

"I didn't know. I *did* know that I didn't know. I was so damn confused."

"I'd have straightened you out." There was a hint of heat in Connor's words.

"Oh, I don't know about straight..." he shot back. This was what he'd missed over the last few weeks.

"No, you're right about that. But you'd have been a lot

less confused, I can promise you that. I wonder if she could tell? Women are smart like that."

"Yeah. She was a good friend. She covered for me a couple of times, then I came out to my folks." Early remembered how calm they both had been, how he'd been so scared, and Momma and Pop had simply asked if he had someone they needed to meet.

"I know that story. One of many reasons they're the best in-laws ever."

"They are. That and Momma makes good French toast."

Jayden came up to the edge of the pool. "Glad you're home, Dad. I missed you."

"I missed you too. I just—you know what?" Shockingly, Connor jumped up, stripped off his T-shirt and PJ bottoms and jumped in the pool in his undies.

"Dad!"

Connor just laughed and chased Jayden across the pool.

Oh. Fucking A.

Early loved it. Joy was a perfect look—on his husband and his sons.

Jaxson climbed on Connor's back, and they zoomed around the shallow end, while Jayden showed off his underwater handstands. He'd finished his coffee before Connor finally glanced his direction again. He got a big grin and a shrug.

"I have time to shower before family day, right?"

"Absolutely. You look great in there, darlin'."

"Boss! Boss, we got horses out!"

"Dammit." He bit the word out. "Get them in and fix the fence. I want you to put two men on riding fence. I want to know what's going on."

"Everything okay?" Connor moved toward the steps to get out of the pool. "Did he say the horses were out?"

"Yeah. We've got a fence problem. Goodie." Early rolled his eyes. "I think it's just weak spots the guys were being lazy checking."

"It's tough being the boss." Fortunately Connor's undies were tighty and black, not white, so they weren't obscene wet. "You need to go see what's up? I'll pull the kids out of the pool for a quick shower."

"Yeah, if you don't mind. I'm going to have a chat with the guys, do a little encouraging." He stood and stretched, back popping.

"Go ahead. I've got this. I'm only a little out of practice." Connor kissed his cheek. "Go be a cowboy."

"Yes, sir. You go be a dad, and in a few hours, we'll go be a family." And he was going to be over the moon.

15

Connor sat down on a bench in the shade and took a big swig from a bottle of water. It wasn't terribly cold, but he didn't care. That potato sack race took it out of him, and he was thirsty.

It would have been fine if they'd done a family race, because he could have hung back with Jaxson and just hopped along until they finally crossed the finish line. But no, they'd set up a "Dad's race". So he was lined up next to a bunch of cowboys, including his husband, who took this whole potato sack thing way too seriously.

He hadn't come close to winning, but he'd been toward the front of the pack, he hadn't fallen, and he'd even gotten applause from people he didn't even know as he finished.

"Early! Introduce us to your guy!"

All these people came to meet him—mostly women, but there were a handful of men, plus Chay, the pretty Navajo man they'd met after the funeral.

Early introduced him to every single person that asked.

And there were many.

A lot.

Jesus Christ, Early knew everyone. It was exhausting, and he wasn't going to remember anyone's name. And it was ridiculously intimidating because these weren't just acquaintances—these were friends of Early's parents, friends of Early's from school, his kids' friends' parents. Teachers. Neighbors.

"This is exhausting," he said out loud, and then sighed because he hadn't meant to. And there wasn't much chance that Early hadn't heard him.

Early blinked over, eyes widened for half a second before he spoke. "If you want, there's a coffee shop a block down and over. I can come pick you up with the boys once they're done."

"What?" He glanced at Early. Did his husband really think he'd just go have coffee and leave his family here? "I didn't mean the event. Not at all. I'm having a great time. I love seeing everything the boys have been doing. It's just... meeting all these people. You seem to know everyone, and I feel like I'm walking into this enormous...life. I'm having trouble keeping up."

"Okay, how can I help?" Early bumped shoulders with him, giving him a wink. "You want me to build you a fort? We got juice boxes."

He shook his head, eyes rolling, but Early had managed to make him smile, right? "You're an idiot. Yes, please. Can you build it around the hot tub?"

"Oh, that's a good—"

"Daddy? Dad? Can we spend the night at Jack and Daniel's tonight and they come to our house tomorrow night?" Jayden ran up with his brother and a pair of red-headed, freckled twins.

"Uh. Jack and Daniel?" Cute. He looked at Early. "You know their parents?"

"I do. Lauren and... Mike? He's a fireman. She's a librarian. Right, boys?"

"Right, Mr. Early!"

"Momma says it's fine—"

"With you if it's—"

"All right with her!"

Wow. Twins. "It's okay with me," he said softly, just for Early's ears. He wasn't going to say yes without Early's buy in.

"All right, boys. Let me talk with your Momma, but I think we can work it out." Early winked at them as they ran away, hooting and hollering. "I figure a night alone in the hot tub is good, right?"

"It's exactly what we need." It was worth having a house full of boys tomorrow. He took a breath. "Exactly."

"Perfect. A bottle of wine, some pizza, the hot tub, good music, and us." Early nodded. "And the moving truck comes tomorrow, so the twins can occupy the boys while we mess with our stuff."

"I could kiss you right now." He wouldn't, because this wasn't the venue for that kind of thing. "But I'll be patient. The truck comes tomorrow? Already. I'm looking forward to moving our things in."

"It will help make the house ours, you know?"

He rested a hand on Early's back; surely that was mild enough for a family gathering. The touch grounded him, reminded him why he was here. Made him feel less disoriented. "Is this what it was like when you moved to Denver?"

"A little, yeah. I felt like the whole world was changed—new and exciting, but unnerving and hard." Early shrugged, head tilting like he did when he was remembering something. "I had you, though, and you are my true north."

He nodded. "Yeah. Yes, to all of that." And he'd never known that Early was unhappy—or, at least not as happy as he could have been, because Early was so obviously happy now. "Plus the law firm doesn't do potato sack races to break the ice. That was awesome."

"Well, we are living the mountain town life now." Early met his eyes. "I'm going to work hard to make you crazy happy."

"Well, I guess I'd better work extra hard to appreciate that." He gave Early a suggestive wink. "I'll get started on that tonight."

"Mmhmm... First, let me introduce you to the twins' mom. You'll talk to her a lot." Early rolled his eyes. "A lot, a lot."

"Ah, one of *those*." He was okay with that. He had the mom thing down. "Moms love me."

"They do. She's the children's librarian. She knows a little bit about everything. Her husband's a stud."

"Librarians always get the hot ones." He chuckled. "What does he do again?"

"Firefighter. So he's one day on and two days off. I try to make sure she's never left with all four boys when he's not home."

"She's got four? Damn, okay. More is easier anyway." Parenting was much easier when the boys had friends over to keep them entertained. "I'm game."

"No. No, I meant her twins and our boys. Although..."

An obviously pregnant woman walked up, red hair curling around her face. "Looks like we're sharing children again."

Early laughed right out loud. "Yes, ma'am. Lauren, this is my man, Connor."

"Hey, Connor. I'm Lauren. It's so good to meet you."

Connor shook hands with her gently. "Good to meet you. Those boys of yours are adorable."

"They're a handful. Especially now." She laughed as she patted her belly. "I bet you're glad to finally be here, huh?"

"You have no idea." Connor sighed, smiling. "It's been a hard summer."

"I bet. I can't imagine not having Mike around. He's got the boys, by the way. They're wanting to go play gooney golf and have corn dogs and watch movies tonight."

"A night off for Mom! He's a keeper. If he really doesn't mind hauling ours around tonight, we'll happily take yours tomorrow night. Send bathing suits."

"Oh, absolutely. Mike got some pool toys to donate to the "exhausting our sons" camp." Lauren winked at him. "Early has been a lifesaver, and the twins are over the moon to have friends."

Connor glanced at Early affectionately. "He is a lifesaver. And I'm sure our boys feel the same way about friends, being new around here."

"Oh, they're both a hoot. They're going to be favorites once school starts, no doubt." Lauren chuckled. "Such cuties."

"Thank you. We'll see. They can be a handful, especially Jax. I guess you have our number? When should we bring the boys by?"

"I'll just keep them, rather than make you two drive out to the ranch and back into town. I know I have at least three outfits apiece of theirs at the house."

When had his boys who needed their special blankets and pillows become boys that had changes of clothes at other people's homes? "Yeah? Great, okay." He leaned closer to Lauren. "I have to say, I'm looking forward to a night to ourselves."

"After a whole week together alone? What were you two doing?"

"Packing. Boxes. Packing so many boxes. It was stressful, you know? I need some time in the hot tub." He grinned and stood up again, giving Early another quick look. "It's just good to be home."

"Oh, I bet. We'll have to have a cookout soon and invite you all. We'd love to introduce you around."

"That sounds nice. Early loves a cookout, don't you, honey?" They'd been babbling all this time, and Early had just been standing there with this sweet smile on his face, listening.

"I do. Man burn meat." Early winked at her, then waggled his eyebrows. "Just tell us when and where."

"And what we can bring."

Lauren nodded. "We'll plan it. It was great meeting you, Connor. We'll see you both tomorrow."

"Thanks, Lauren. Go get off your feet." Connor gave her a wave as she waddled off. "Sounds like we have bonus twins."

"We do. The boys love them to death. They're good, solid kiddos."

"So...who else do I need to meet before we escape?"

"I think we just need to go tell the boys we'll see them tomorrow. That ought to fill you up on meeting new folks." Early's wink was playful as hell.

"I do better one on one." Early was so proud to introduce him to people, he loved that about his man. It was probably nice to finally have another half here like nearly everyone else. He bumped hips with Early and looked around for their boys.

"Mike is six-six, bald, hard to miss. Our boys will be there."

Sure enough, there was a man whose bald head moved through the crowd, and the four boys followed along behind.

"Little ducklings." He chuckled and made his way over, working his way through people. Mike looked taller and taller the closer they got. "Hey, there. You're Mike?"

"I am! You're Connor. Pleased." Mike shook hands with him. "Lauren says we're having our little shared custody weekend again."

"Seems so. Your boys are adorable. They look just like you, just...a lot shorter."

"Less bald for sure." Mike gave him a big grin.

"They say baldness is a sign of virility," Early shot over, and Mike laughed, the sound loud and long.

"I mean, by the looks of your wife..." Connor winked at Mike.

"She's going to have a baby, Dad."

Connor schooled his features and smiled at Jaxson, but it wasn't easy. "I know. Isn't that amazing?"

"Yeah, I guess. Are you going to adopt more kids, Dad? I mean, the house is big."

"Oh, uh..." He glanced at Early, then back at Mike. "Well, we haven't talked about that." He wanted more—a couple more even—and he had a feeling Early would be on board, but adopt? Maybe. Maybe a surrogate. A bigger family had been on his mind a lot in those long hours alone in Denver.

"Son, that's a family talk, okay? If you want to talk about it later, we will."

Jayden nodded at him, grinned. "I wouldn't mind a little brother."

"You could get a little sister." Mike pointed at his wife, who was chatting with some friends a few feet away.

"A girl? Congratulations." A girl would be great. Maybe they could have this conversation later.

"Oh..." Jayden seemed so disappointed, but Jaxson bounced.

"Girls are okay. They are pretty, but we want puppies first!"

Jayden's eyes lit up. "Right!"

"Oh, that is definitely a family conversation." Mike laughed and waved to the boys. "Come on, let's get those sno-cones. Go enjoy your time off, guys."

"We'll be home tomorrow, Dad." Jayden offered him a grin and a wave, and Jaxson hugged him hard, then they were gone.

Boom.

"It's weird, huh?" Early said, eyes following them as they walked off.

"Yeah." He nodded, also watching the boys go. "But good weird."

"It is." Early grabbed his hand. "Come on. You want a fancy coffee before we go home?"

"Fancy coffee—yes please." He followed Early toward the parking lot. "We get to hold hands? Aren't we going to scandalize people?" He was joking...mostly.

Early shot him a wide-eyed look. "I've been out for a long time. I'm not living somewhere I can't be your husband, and I won't raise our boys somewhere we have to hide."

He rolled his eyes, indulgently. "Well, don't look at me like that. When I met you, you didn't do anything but look hot as fuck in public. How do I know how things work here?"

"You know how I work. You ought to know that I wouldn't make you feel less than, even for the ranch."

He did, of course. Maybe he just needed his feathers

smoothed out some. A little validation. It wasn't like him to feel insecure. "I know. But thank you for reminding me anyway." He squeezed Early's fingers as they got to the sidewalk.

"Come on. We could both use something sweet and cold and caffeinated." They headed down toward the train station, the little coffee shop waiting at the corner. It smelled like hazelnut and caramel and coffee and chocolate.

"Oh, it smells like civilization in here," he teased. "What a cute place." It wasn't anything special, it was just a cute, tiny little place for tourists, but it felt cozy and smelled amazing.

"Right? I want an iced caramel latte with whipped cream." Early grinned at Connor. "And a brownie."

His man was so fucking cute sometimes. "Oh, we're going there are we? Then I'm having the same with an extra shot, and an oatmeal raisin cookie."

"Oh, I like you two!" A young woman with colorful locs smiled at him. "I have a great apple turnover too."

"Tempting." He nodded. "Next time." It did sound good though. "I love all your color."

"Thanks. Jen at Shear Perfection did it. You could totally rock this look."

Oh, no. He couldn't imagine. "Ha. Thank you. I don't know that I have that in me."

"See how you feel when you're caffeinated." She was making their drinks while she talked, looking every bit as practiced as his city barista, but much more relaxed.

"Oh, anything could happen with enough caffeine."

Early's eyes were as big as saucers, but the laughter was just barely held in.

"Don't worry, honey, I'm not dyeing my hair."

Another barista put plates with their sweets on them on

the bar, and he reached for them. "Let's get a seat by the window?"

"Totally. We can watch the tourists. You missed the bike rally."

"Bicycles? Were there a lot of people?"

"Motorcycles, and lots of leather. Lots. I drove down to watch." Early's wink was pure naughtiness.

"Whoa. I can't wait until next year. Maybe I'll buy myself a jacket so you don't have to wait that long for leather."

Early's smile blossomed over his entire face. "Mmm... that would be nice for the fall, wouldn't it? My studly leather lawyer?"

Studly? He didn't think he was the stud in this relationship, but the way Early appreciated his suggestion made his spine tingle. "I don't have to wear a suit on a regular basis anymore, so I'm looking forward to extending my wardrobe."

"Mmm...jeans. Your butt looks fine in denim." Wasn't that a happy sound?

"Jeans, T-shirt, leather jacket, boots... I should get some boots." Now he was playing with Early, but he kind of did want boots.

"Hell, yes. Biker boots and cowboy boots both." Early was right there, into it.

"You look like you might cream your jeans if I asked for a Harley for Christmas." He grinned and stuck the straw to his iced coffee between his teeth.

Early lit up like it was the Fourth of July. "Your birthday is before that..."

"You want to buy me a bike?" He laughed. "Come on. I mean a bike would be cool but...me?" Something was wrong with him. He actually didn't hate the idea. He was kind of intrigued now.

"Why not? You're the hottest bastard I've ever seen." Early leaned forward. "I could snuggle up behind you, hold your hips as you ride."

"You really like this idea? Maybe I'll try one out. I've never ridden one." But he could learn. He needed a hobby. There was a lot of open road where they lived.

"I haven't either, but I love the visual of you straddling a Harley, waiting for me."

"It sounds so Top Gun." He chuckled. But it was a plan now, even if they didn't buy one he'd make that little fantasy happen for his husband. Why not? "Let's find me a truck first. My BMW isn't built for a ranch."

"Yeah—did you want a pickup or something like a long wheelbase Range Rover, so you can haul many boys?"

"Ooh a Range Rover. Swanky." In a nice steel blue or black. That would be sweet. "Hauling boys will be key, obviously."

"Yep. Hauling boys, taking me on dates—all the good bits." Early beamed at him. "Speaking of good bits...that hot tub and childless evening is calling to us."

"We could get up to no good in a Range Rover for sure. Are you done with your brownie? I think you're wearing half of it."

"You were the one teasing me about a Harley."

"Point taken. Tell you what." He leaned across the table as he stood up. "I'll lick all that chocolate off you when we get home."

"I have a bottle of Hershey's in the fridge."

Early seemed dead serious. That was amusing. And strangely hot. "You want some sticky fun after the hot tub? I'm in. Then we can shower too. We can tell the kids we had ice cream. Come on, cowboy."

"Right behind you, darlin'. Let's go play."

16

"Boss! I need you to sign off on this before you go into your new interview!"

"Boss! I need you to call that woman that runs the feed store and approve my changes!"

"Boss!"

"Boss!"

"Boss!"

Lord have mercy, Early was going to change his name.

He went to grab another cup of coffee, frowning when he found the pot empty. "Oh, dammit."

"Already on it." Connor crossed the kitchen with the coffee in his hand. "We were out, I had to get some from the big pantry." A week until school started, and Connor was looking like he'd spent the whole summer on the ranch. He was in boots and jeans and had a decent sunburn that was turning to tan. "Your phone's been ringing all morning, huh?"

"Since five friggin' thirty. How are the hooligans?" They were probably in the pool again or still. Whichever.

"I pulled them out of the pool a half an hour ago, and

I'm making them read. Good call finding that summer reading list for the new school. They have to sit still for an hour or so. How many for lunch do you think?"

"I'd say none, but the way my phone's been going? At least a couple extra. Demming's worried I won't find a replacement—" But it was hard, knowing this would be someone who was going to be running things, be around his children.

"So...be honest with me. How much work is Demming actually doing now that you're here?"

"Not much anymore. I've been trying to make sure we can handle it if I can't find someone."

Connor nodded. "I figured. So we can manage until you find the right person. I'm not freelancing much yet, so you can put me to work if you need to once the kids are in school. I'm game." The coffee maker seemed to be taking forever.

"I—" He shook his head and stepped closer, like they weren't alone. "I've never hired folks before, and Demming's been here forever, you know?"

"You're not throwing him out, honey. He wants to retire. He's ready. Have you asked him to help interview? Have you taken ads out anywhere? You want me to ask around someplace?"

"I have ads out in some of the trade magazines, and he sits in if someone gets through the first interview." There'd been two of them—one decided he didn't like the money, and the second interviewee had been great, but she'd never called back.

"I'm sorry this is frustrating." Connor kissed his cheek just as the coffee began to gurgle. "Oh. Coffee. Yay."

"Me too. I have another interview today. Want to sit in?" He'd feel better if Connor did, he thought.

"Yeah, sure. I can do that. When is it?" Connor took his mug and filled it up. "I just need to make sure the boys are occupied."

"Right after lunch. We can make them sit and search the puppies in the shelters." That would occupy them for an hour. At least.

They'd print out a ream of puppy pictures, but it would keep them busy.

"I like how you think." Connor touched their mugs together, toasting.

"I wish that one applicant would have taken me up on the job. She and her wife were good people."

"Do you know why she didn't?"

"No. She just sort of...stopped returning my calls." It had been weird as hell, really.

"You want me to reach out? I could follow up, see if I can figure out what's up." Connor sipped his coffee and leaned on the counter. "Turn on my lawyer charm."

"Honestly? I would love that. She was a great fit, married to a kindergarten teacher. They liked the house. You know, that whole thing."

"Weird. Maybe she got a better offer. Anyway, text me her number, I'll give her a call and she if she'll have coffee with me." Connor chuckled. "Send me your max salary figure too."

"I just took ten thousand off what Demming is making. That seemed fair."

"So, if it's about the money I can offer her ten more?" Connor grinned at him.

"Do you think that's the right thing to do?" He wasn't sure how that worked, honestly. They'd have to be worth what Demming was...

"Maybe, if the money is the reason she can't take the job. Demming's not really supporting a family or anything, right? You're a new owner, so this is a kind of new business. I think it's more about what the ranch can afford, and what the right person is worth to you than what Demming was making."

"Yeah, I guess. I liked her ideas, I liked that they want to stay, raise a family." He was tickled about it, in fact, and Demming had been too.

"I think if hiring her is more than just someone that can get the job done, then make her a sweet offer. Text me a salary you think she's worth."

"Okay. But, I mean, if she decided she didn't like the place, she didn't." And that hurt his feelings, weirdly enough. This place was—well, he'd uprooted his whole family for it, hadn't he?

Connor snorted. "The ranch? There's no way she didn't like it. It's gorgeous and well-run. It's something else. Maybe her dog died. Maybe her marriage is on the rocks. Maybe she got a really good offer somewhere else. But it's not the ranch."

"Right, because this is an amazing place to be." Connor was right. "So, we have lunch, an interview. What else is on our list?"

Besides answering the phone twenty-seven times an hour.

"I have to take the boys school shopping. I got the list— but they also need sneakers. They're fine with clothes until the weather gets colder, Jayden's pants are too short. And you said you'd show me how to deal with the pool chemicals so you don't have to, and—hang on." Connor pulled his phone out and squinted at it. "And...okay. And I'm apparently going to a PTO meeting this afternoon. Kids can come; it's at the school. Text from Mike, who says he doesn't want to be the only dad there."

Mike and Connor were building a solid little friendship, and Early loved it. Mike knew everyone in town, and was more than willing to fold Connor in.

"Excellent. If you want me to come shopping this evening and have supper out, we can." He needed some shampoo and a couple of heavy flannel shirts.

"That sounds great. We can each take a boy and a list and get it done faster. And dinner out means no dishes." Connor kissed him again. "You're brilliant."

"I've been told that before." Early winked at his husband, before cracking up. "You want Mexican? Burgers? Italian?"

"Mexican. Tacos. Definitely tacos. And a huge margarita."

"Ooh... I'm in. So, interview. I'll come to town with you post-meeting, we'll shop, have tacos and tequila, then put the boys to bed so we can have a late-night swim?"

"Perfect and text me that name and number, I'm going to call her. This morning."

Early topped them both off and set the carafe back down. "Go do. I'm going to check on the kids. And hey. I love you."

Connor's smile was warm, tickling the shit out of him. "I love you too, darlin'."

Early's phone rang again, and he pulled it out of his pocket.

"Good luck!" Connor chuckled and headed out onto the porch.

"Yeah, yeah. Hey, Demming, what's up?"

"Well, boss, I got to tell you—"

And he was off and running.

Again.

17

Early was right. Their kids were part fish. Not five minutes after their reading break and the two of them were back in the pool. Connor loved that they got so much time outdoors and so much exercise, it wore them out and they slept as hard as they played.

He had his laptop set up on the poolside table and was sitting in the shade under the goofy tropical umbrella that Early had found. It was so hideous it was just perfect. He'd been working with his former firm, wrapping up the cases he'd had pending when he moved, so he wasn't completely without something to do, but there was no rush on it, so he figured now was as good a time as any for that phone call.

He looked at the text from Early that said her name was Reese and had a cell number and a salary that was a little bit higher than he'd expected. That was a last resort, but it was good to have it in his back pocket if that was the only reason she'd stopped taking Early's calls.

The boys were laughing, but the sound was swallowed up by the vastness of the open air out here so it was only background level. He dialed the number, wondering if

Reese was the type that screened or picked up calls from numbers she didn't know. He was a screener, so he'd understand.

It rang for a few, then he got a breathless, "'lo? Watch that heifer, y'all! Don't you let him slip by you!"

"Hello, this is Connor Westin calling, am I speaking with Reese Morrow?" It sounded like maybe this was a bad time.

"Yep. Do I know you? Oops. Just a sec." There was a terrible clang and then a soft chuckle. "Sorry. Back."

He forged ahead. "I'm Early Jericho's husband from the Rocking Bar M. I'm so sorry to bother you when you're obviously busy, do you think you might have some time to talk later? Or maybe meet for coffee?"

"I was just penning calves. What's up?" There was the tiniest hint of anger that he didn't understand in her voice.

"Well, Early was telling me about you—how impressed he was with your interview and how much he liked you as a person...he was surprised when he didn't hear back from you, so I thought I'd follow up to see if you have any questions, or maybe just ask you why you decided you weren't interested?" He couldn't imagine what Early might have done to upset her, everything Early said was so positive.

There was a pause, then, "Are you serious? Dude, you're being played. His lover is getting the job. The bastard told me—your husband didn't even have the class to call me himself. Ass."

"His—" What the hell? He couldn't imagine how she'd heard a story so completely off. His lover? "I don't know who fed you that bullshit but trust me when I tell you I am the only lover he needs. And we're nowhere near hiring anyone yet, the only person he's even considered so far is you." Okay, he was pissed off now. All the little hairs were standing up on the back of his neck. This was his husband's name someone was fucking with. "Early is the most honest man you'll ever meet, so if anyone's an ass it's the fucker that lied to you."

"Wait... You're sure? I mean, you're sure he's not cheating?"

Just the word "cheating" got his hackles up. "I am a hundred percent sure. Period. He loves his family. He loves me. I'd like to know who thinks they're getting the job though, because Early wants to offer it to you."

"Oh... Oh, dammit. Okay. Okay, we need to meet, I think. You and me and Mr. Early, because that Ian guy said the job was his and to back off."

"I apologize for that." What the fuck? He wouldn't trust Ian to foreman his morning dump. His heart pounded and heat crept up his neck as he felt his blood pressure rise. *Ian.* That scheming little bastard. He made himself breathe. He needed to keep it together until they hung up. "Why don't you come out to the ranch in the morning?"

"Sure. Sure, no problem. I thought Mr. Early was a good guy. I was disappointed as all get out."

"So was he when he didn't hear from you. I look forward to meeting you and hopefully clearing up this misunderstanding."

"What time should I be there? I'll bring doughnuts."

"Around nine? Early likes the jelly ones and we have two boys who will be looking for glazed. As long as you're asking," he joked. She had definitely not asked.

"I'm assuming the Ian guy isn't hanging around the ranch, then? Because I'm grumpy that he almost lost me my dream job."

Early was going to be happy to hear that. "He better not

be, or I'll have his goddamn balls. Excuse my French." Oh, he was so pissed.

"Oh, I like you. I like you already. I'll be there tomorrow at nine with doughnuts. You provide the coffee."

"I'll put the good stuff on. Thank you for taking my call. See you tomorrow." He hung up, caught between excited to tell Early that Reese was coming by, and royally ticked that he had to tell Early about that slimeball, Ian.

Also, he needed to know whether Ian was still...here, somehow. Not here on the ranch because clearly he wasn't, but here causing trouble.

"Dad? You okay?" Jaxson was at the edge of the pool, looking at him curiously.

He schooled his expression, finding a great big smile. "I'm great. I think we found a foreman to help Daddy run the ranch. Are you a big ol' prune yet?"

"Nope. I can't believe this is our house. Is it cool for you too?"

"It's very cool, buddy. I can't really believe it either. Are you ready to do some school shopping tonight? I got the list from your teacher."

He heard Jayden's groan from across the pool. "How is summer almost over already?"

"I get it." He'd lost his summer to packing and moving and missing his family. But he was really looking forward to fall. "Daddy's taking us out for tacos after."

"Yeah? I like tacos. Cool. Papaw says that maybe we can go to the movies with him this weekend if it's okay."

"I can't see why not. Maybe Mamaw will want you to stay the night."

"Yeah, she likes hanging out. I like seeing them whenever we want. Do you like it too?"

He walked over and sat on the concrete by the edge of

the pool. It seemed like there was something going on with his boys, something maybe they'd talked about. "Are you guys really that worried I'm not going to like it here?"

"Yeah, because—" Jaxson started, and Jayden splashed him, stopping the flow of words.

"We just want you to like it."

He nodded to Jayden. "I like it. Listen you guys. Daddy spent a long time in Denver because I wanted to be there. He loves this ranch, and it's my turn to be where he wants to be, that's all. I'm not going anywhere. I don't love Daddy any less. Actually, I may even love him more. And you guys are the most important thing to both of us."

"Daddy told Papaw that he was scared he was making you unhappy," Jaxson blurted out.

"Jaxson! Shut up!" Jayden pushed Jaxson, making his brother flail. "Jesus, you always tell *everything*."

"Jayden," he said sharply. "Don't talk that way to your brother. Come here, Jax." He helped Jaxson climb out of the pool. "Come over here, Jay." He waited until his boys were settled. "Grownups aren't perfect, including me and your daddy. We're going to make mistakes and worry whether we made the right decisions about things, just like you guys do. But he and I are a team. The four of us are a team too. So I appreciate you looking out for me."

Jayden stared at him, so, so serious. "We just—this is a great place, and we can ride horses and swim and everything, but I asked Daddy, and he said if you are unhappy, we will go back to Denver. He says he loves you more than the ranch."

Jaxson pushed in. "But this house is big enough for more kids, Dad. We could get a baby and puppies, and I'm going to do 4H and everything, so you're going to be so busy getting to be dad, and you won't miss any of it!"

He fought tears, partly because he hadn't fully understood what Early was going through, but mostly because he was so touched by his boys. He was raising these two kind, thoughtful people. This was the good stuff right here. This was what parenting was about.

That, and the fact that he was going to have to change because Jaxson basically just used his T-shirt as a towel.

"You want to know a secret? I have never seen Daddy so happy. Have you? And I've never seen the two of you so tan and busy having fun either. How could I not love it here?" He was still adjusting, but the boys needed reassurance and he had plenty of that.

"Daddy is so busy, and he never has a headache anymore. If he looks sad, he just goes and loves on the horses or jumps in the pool or we go and play with the goats. He smiles all the time." Jaxson beamed at him, and Connor just melted.

"The best is when we have ideas now." Jayden's eyes were wide.

He completely agreed with Jaxson, and marveled at how observant he was. Kids really did pay attention. "Oh yeah? What ideas?"

"Like he wants to make a room in the basement that's like a movie theater, and he's letting us help. He says it should be a family project."

"Oh, I love that idea. Do you want couches or reclining seats?"

He couldn't wait to talk to Early. About this, about Reese, even about that bastard Ian. Early needed to know he was on board, hear it directly from him like the kids did. "All right, everyone get a towel, and go rinse off. We need to make lunch and then Daddy and I have a project for you while we have a meeting later."

"And then we're going to have tacos and buy new backpacks!" Jaxson cheered and both the boys ran for the towels. It was amazing to see them—the boys had never been idle, but Early made sure they never had time for real mischief.

It was nice to see them excited to start at their new school. He couldn't wait for school to begin so he'd have some time to think about what was next for him, and what role he could play in this whole ranch business.

But first, an interview they hopefully weren't going to need, then tacos and margaritas.

18

Shopping had been hilarious, the tacos had been perfect, and Connor had loved the margaritas.

Not bad for an evening.

The boys had gone down with their books without a fuss, and he went downstairs to get himself a beer. "You want a beer, darlin'?"

"Yes, please and thank you. You want to drink it on the porch?" Connor followed him down.

"Totally. That was fun with the boys, wasn't it?" He wasn't sure shopping for school had ever been entertaining before.

"Jaxson's got some opinions, let me tell you. No superhero backpack for him anymore. That fatigue thing is something else. And don't even suggest that purple was ever his favorite color."

"He's not a baby anymore, Da-Aa-ad." Early did a fine Jaxson impersonation if he did say so himself.

Connor rewarded him with a laugh as they took their beers out onto the porch. "And Jayden...when did everything have to be black and white? And when did his feet get so damn big?"

"I blame the pool. No shoes, so they just get to swell uncontrollably." It was as good an excuse as any, right?

"Yeah, okay, cowboy." Connor snorted and sat. "So, speaking of the pool...the boys had an important discussion with me this morning."

"Yeah?" He popped the top of Connor's beer and handed it over. "What about? They worried about school?"

"No, they were worried about *me*. It's very important to them that I like it here. They wanted to make sure I was happy. Seems they overheard a conversation between you and your dad."

Early frowned. "A what? What did they hear?"

What had he said? He'd worried about Connor, sure, but he hadn't said anything bad about that. He knew it.

"Jayden said you told your dad you were worried you were making me unhappy." Connor was watching him closely.

"Well, sure. I was. I am. But I told him, straight out, if you weren't happy here, we'd go back to Denver. You're my heart."

"They told me that too." Connor grinned at him. "They don't want to go back to Denver. Jaxson had a whole speech for me about why the ranch is so cool, and Jayden added some more practical reasons too. It was so sweet."

"Oh. Oh, lord. You scared me. I thought they'd totally misunderstood something I'd said." He took a deep swig of his beer. "I mean, I'm sorry that they were worried, and they shouldn't eavesdrop, but at least I did say it."

"I'm sure it was tougher than it seemed on them to have us split up all summer. Kids worry. But I didn't know I'd worried you so much."

He shrugged, because what was he going to say? "You gave up a lot to come here, and I know it. This is my dream, my fantasy, not yours."

"Hm. Denver was never a dream or a fantasy for me, honey. But you are. I'm ready for this adventure, I promise."

Early reached out and squeezed his husband's fingers. "Thank God for that, darlin'. Seriously."

He couldn't believe this was his life. Not at all.

Connor squeezed back. "I love you; you know that. We're going to figure all of this out." Connor sipped his beer. "Even the foreman situation."

"You said she's coming back in the morning? Did she say why she'd changed her mind?" He couldn't imagine what had happened that she'd ghost him and then agree to come back in.

"Yeah." Connor nodded slowly, sipped his beer, taking his time getting it out. "Ian."

"Who?" He tilted his head, trying to suss that out. Ian. Did he even know an Ian? Wait. "You mean chocolate cake Ian?"

"Yes. The one that told me he was the nanny? He told Reese..." Connor shook his head. "Early. He told Reese the job was his."

Early actually dropped his beer in utter shock, and it took him a second to figure out what that bang and whoosh noise was. "Dammit!"

Connor hopped up and slid the little table between them out of the way. "Did it break?"

"No. No, shit. Fuck. I just. Fuck!" Ian wasn't a cowboy. Not even a little bit. Why would the son of a bitch want the foreman job?

"Reese was pissed, understandably, that you hadn't told her yourself. He's after you, Early. I told you. And now he's

fucking with your reputation? I'm ready to cut his balls off."
Connor kept his cool, saying that like it was just a fact.

"Okay. You have my support." And his confusion. What
the hell was the little shit's deal?

Connor nodded and "I think when we talk to Reese we
need to hire her, and then make a plan. I don't trust him not
to show up again. He's fucking with your business now, you
know? It's not just a prank."

"I just don't understand, Connor. I mean, this is
ridiculous."

"What don't you understand, honey?" Connor looked at
him like he had two heads. "He's got the hots for you, and
you're taken. Somewhere in his head he's decided you
deserve to be fucked with. I just can't believe that nutjob was
anywhere near my children. And your parents. It's
terrifying."

"But..." He rolled his eyes. He was a middle-aged dad,
who was taken and busy. He didn't need this shit. "I might
just beat him myself."

"Good. I like that we're on the same page. Reese is too.
Trust me. I think she really wants this." Connor fixed the
table and slid his beer over to him to sip. "She's even
bringing doughnuts."

"I like doughnuts..." His mind was still working on the
fact that someone was screwing with him, his ranch, his
husband. "He seemed so damn decent."

"Where did he come from? Where did you meet him? I
mean...how did you end up hiring him in the first place?"
Connor watched him. "Did someone you know recommend
him?"

Early frowned, trying to remember. "I think... I think
that one of the hands suggested him to work on the yard, do
handyman stuff?"

"Can you reach him? Do you have a number?"

"In my phone, yeah. I haven't called him since I let him go, though. He didn't even come and pick up his last paycheck, as far as I know."

"That's...weird. Text me that number. I might call that bastard tomorrow."

"Sure." He wasn't going to do a single goddamn thing that would let Connor believe for a second that he had something to hide.

Connor put a hand on his thigh. "That's enough about him. I've got your back, honey. You just run your ranch."

"Yeah?" Those words were like a promise, and that touch was everything. "Thank you."

"You're welcome. I told the kids today we're a team. You and me, us and them. That's what we do." Connor slid out of his chair and offered him a hand up. "Let's call it a night."

"Let me spray the beer off the deck, and I'll be right in." He shot Connor a smile. "Wanna have a nice long shower?"

"I was just thinking what I need is a really good...shower. I'll meet you upstairs." Connor grabbed his T-shirt and tugged him in close. "Don't make me wait too long I might have to start without you."

"I wouldn't dare." He leaned in, holding Connor's gaze.

Their kiss was all heat and promise, but Connor cut it short, leaving him on the porch with a mess to clean up.

19

A shower was a great idea. Connor was ready to scrub every thought of that Ian guy off his husband's muscled body and wash the name right out of his own mouth with Early's hot prick.

He started the water, hung towels on the warmer and set the lighting just how they liked it. He loved everything about this bathroom. It was bigger than Jaxson's little bedroom back in Denver, and Early had spared no expense on the shower.

He's been kind of iffy on shower sex before—their shower in Denver was a little tight, the showerhead was in a weird place—but now? It was a favorite. Even more than the hot tub.

He stripped off his shirt and kicked off his shoes, taking his time so he didn't get too far ahead of his man. But he'd be happy to wait under that spray, give Early something to look at.

He heard Early in the bedroom, and he smiled as music filled the air—something slow and sexy that throbbed for him.

He left his jeans with everything else and stepped into the shower, then he swiped his hand across the fogged-up glass to give Early a sneak peek from the bathroom doorway. *How about that, cowboy?*

Was that a moan? He was pretty sure that was a moan.

Connor stretched up as tall as he could.

Oh, yeah. That was a moan.

God, he loved turning Early on. That kind of rush never got old. "Are you coming in, honey?"

"You know it, darlin'." The door opened, and his lover stood there, hard and proud and focused on him.

It was the focus that got him every time. Early made his knees weak with that look. "Mmm. I am a lucky man." Connor held his hand out. "Come give me some of that."

"All of it." Early stepped in, bringing their bodies together with a soft, happy little sigh. "Oh damn, darlin', you do it for me."

"Yeah, well. You make it easy." He slid a hand around Early's nape and kissed him, knowing Early was all his, but working for it anyway.

Early groaned, one hand curling around his ass like it belonged there. He remembered that—how delicious it had been the first time they danced, and Early's hand had found its place unfailingly.

"Mm." Dancing. They needed to do that soon. He swayed a little, making sure their hips were close enough to rub and keep Early wanting. "Did you work hard today, cowboy? Maybe I have a reward for you."

"This morning was tough." Early's laugh was heady as hell. "Hard, you know? I was fixin' to lose it."

It would be more believable without the chuckles.

"I meant after we got out of bed." He pinched Early's nipple, then bent and soothed it with his tongue.

"Uh-huh. So hard." Early wasn't really listening; he was feeling with his whole soul, and Connor loved that about him.

"I know, honey." He visited the other nipple with his teeth, and Early grunted, grabbing his head and pulling him closer.

"Fuck me, that's hot."

Of course it was; that was why he did it. Reducing Early to a horny caveman was one of his great joys in life. He found Early's cock and stroked it slowly, teasing. "Hmm. We haven't done that in this shower yet."

"Uh-huh...wanna?" Early's face went slack, and his hips rocked up, driving toward his touch.

"Uh-huh." He looked around the shower. He turned around and offered Early his ass, tucking both hands behind his head and putting on a little show. "That what you want, cowboy?"

"It's always what I want, darlin'." Early didn't miss a beat. Those slick fingers pressed inside him without a hint of hesitation.

"Fuck." He reached out suddenly, both hands scrabbling on the shower wall to brace himself. "Fuck, Early."

"Uh-huh." Biting little kisses covered his upper back, making his toes curl.

Early knew every damn sensitive spot he had, inside and out and he couldn't stop his moan. He pushed back offering more skin for those lips to devour.

Those fingers kept pushing, driving into him, sending him soaring. He arched back, never too self-conscious to ride, whether it was Early's fingers or his prick.

When Early's touch disappeared, he gasped, searching for it again, but Early went and sat on the solid shower seat, slicking his cock.

"That's pretty." Pretty was a playful understatement. The way Early handled his own wood was the hottest thing ever. Connor shifted to lean over his husband, one hand braced on the wall. "Pretty, fat cock. All for me."

"Every inch, darlin'." Early drew him closer. "Want you to ride me."

"I'm ready for you. This way, or that?" He twisted one way and then the other. Facing, or a better view of his ass? "Either way it's yours, you stud of a cowboy."

"I want to be able to kiss you, darlin'. Load on."

"You think you're that hot Harley you're gonna buy me, huh?" He made the best show he could out of straddling Early and reached back to get hold of the slick cock that was waiting for him. "Great big motor humming between my knees." They both got off on a slow burn entry, so he took his time taking Early in, lowering himself little by little.

"Uh-huh. Going to rub against your tight little ass while we ride. Gonna be so hot, darlin'." Early watched him like he was the hottest human alive. How could that little fuck Ian think for a second that Early's heart wasn't taken?

"Hotter than this?" He sank until his ass met Early's thighs, offering Early a satisfied groan. "I don't believe it."

"Nothing is hotter than this. Ever." Early drew him right in for a hard, happy kiss.

Damn right. He stayed still, capturing Early's cock until Early moaned and cursed and he couldn't stand it another second. When he started to move their groans of relief echoed off the tiled walls. It might have been funny if he wasn't so fucking desperate.

Early held his hips, encouraging him to move, to ride him.

He rose up and sank down, quickly picking up the pace.

Connor wasn't feeling patient, he was chasing what he needed and making sure to take Early along with him.

Early's face was an expression of need, of pure hunger that pulled at the corners of his mouth. "Come on, darlin'. Show me how good it is."

He nodded and curled his fingers around Early's nape for balance, shifting so Early's prick stroked just the right spot. "Yes, fuck! So good. Fuck, honey."

Early nodded, lighting him up over and over, totally focused on making him shoot, driving him crazy. He tossed his head back and sucked in air, showing off a little and letting Early push him right to the edge.

One hand wrapped around the tip of his cock, palming the head and working his slit. Pure electricity shot through him, and his entire body tightened.

"Again, again..." But he didn't need another push; he was right there. He pushed up into Early's hand and stars erupted behind his eyelids as he shot.

Early stroked him through his aftershocks before pulling him close and driving into him, a harsh cry splitting the air.

He caught Early's face in his hands and kissed him between rough breaths and deep moans. "You're a fucking stud, and I love you."

"Love you. Damn." Early licked at his lips, lazy and sated, just a little sloppy.

When he felt like his legs would hold him, he slid off Early's lap and moved under the rainfall showerhead, letting the hot water soak his hair and slide over his shoulders. "Mmm. Come on, cowboy. Let's wash up so we can snuggle." Their bed was the next best thing to the shower. It was huge and sturdy and so comfortable. Early had to have spent a fortune on it, but he didn't ask, and he didn't plan to. He loved it.

"Mmhmm... If I can stand. You broke me." Early managed though and leaned on him, slick and heavy.

"You're not broken. You're just out of gas." He winked and got to scrubbing, soaping up all that lovely tanned skin. The one thing they weren't and would never be was broken. It was simply impossible.

"Mmm...putter putter. I love you, darlin'. I'm so glad you're home." Early meant it. He could hear it in that husky voice.

"I know. But you can keep telling me, I don't get tired of hearing it." They had a big day tomorrow so he kept things all business until they were both squeaky clean. "I'm looking forward to tomorrow...getting into how things run around here. If it goes well, I want to work on the budget with your new fore-woman? Foreman? Foreperson?" He shook his head. He could be an idiot sometimes.

"We'll have to ask, but I bet she wants foreman." Early searched his eyes and visibly relaxed. "I would... Oh god, love. I would love that. I don't...well, you know I don't do that so well."

"That's not true, honey; it's just not where your interest lies." He used to think Early was being modest when he said things like that, but over time he learned that his husband actually believed it. Maybe Early was slower than some when it came to money, but he was plenty capable, he just wasn't confident. Early was happier with hands-on work. "I kind of love words and numbers, and I need to feel useful around here, you know? I got this."

"I'm tickled shitless. There are a thousand moving parts to doing this, and I can handle the work if you can help me figure out how to make everything make money like it's supposed to."

"That's kind of an important piece, huh?" They toweled off and he pulled Early to the big bed. "We have *at least* two kids to put through college."

At least.

20

Early was up at five, making coffee and dealing with emails, getting the phone out of the second floor before six when it would start ringing.

Lord have mercy, he had had fun last night. His thighs were letting him know all about it, in fact.

Pretty good, because goddamn, he'd been wound tight to find out that little shit had told Reese he was a liar and a cheat.

A cheat!

Him!

And he'd never done a thing to the kid except ask him to leave after upsetting his husband.

Asshole.

He poured two mugs of coffee at five fifteen and sat them on the table, nodding as Demming came to the back door.

"Boss."

"Hey, Dem. How goes it?" He pushed over a cup and grabbed a pad of paper, getting ready for his daily meeting.

"Great. I am packing, the pod-deal is coming in a week. I may steal the boys. I have a bead on a pair of lab pups that a friend of mine is fostering. One chocolate, one yellow. There's also a Shih Tzu, but I didn't think—"

Oh, Connor would love that. "Can you get them to bring all three? Connor needs a purse dog."

"Oh yeah?" Demming groaned as he sat down. "What kind of purse does he carry?"

He shot back the answer without hesitation. "Pink sequined clutch with a sweet little zebra striped fur trim."

"Ha. You're sure he's a toy dog type? Sounds more like he needs a pretty pony." Demming snorted and picked up his mug. "Thanks for the coffee."

"Of course." He grabbed his pen. "So, dogs, check. What are you doing around nine thirty?"

Demming shrugged. "I guess I'm doing something with you. What's up?"

"That Reese? The one from outside Dallas? She's coming in for a second interview." The woman knew her livestock, and was looking for a long-term position, someplace special.

"Is she? I thought maybe you'd run her off. Good deal."

"Nope. That Ian kid? He told her the job was his. Can you believe that shit?" He sure couldn't.

Demming shook his head. "Why would he want to do that? I thought you ran him off. He sure wasn't getting work here, especially cowboy work."

"I got nothing, man. It doesn't make a lick of sense. I mean, he shit in his own bed with Connor, answering my phone and all. Who answers another man's phone?"

"Unless it's an emergency, no one. You did the right thing sending him on his way. Connor doesn't seem like he'd have much patience for that kind of thing."

He couldn't have stopped his laugh for anything in the world. "Yeah, Connor isn't the most forgiving on that front.

Thank god I don't go out there and flirt with folks. He'd be all butthurt."

"So, how is he...adjusting?"

"He's going to take over the business parts of the operation with me. He'll be way more successful on that front, and he can talk to the BLM folks, that sort of thing. I'm tickled shitless." Connor deserved to feel like he had a place, and there was too much to do as it was, and Early was busy using the expansion permit he'd just secured to separate the mustangs into two herds.

Demming nodded approval. "You'll be a team. That's how it should be."

"Yeah. I think he'll be perfect about it, and it'll leave me to work the land like I want to, and we'll both be able to be full-time dads. It's what I wanted for him." Connor would miss so much otherwise, especially if they adopted another little one.

"Rick would approve." Demming hid behind his coffee mug, about to take a sip. "You know how much he wanted family in this house."

"I didn't. I do now." He met Demming's eyes. "You're sure you want to go to California, man? You want to leave all this?"

"I have grandbabies and a daughter with a beach house. I'm terrified." Demming held his gaze, sure and steady. "Seriously, though, they've been asking me to come for a couple of years. It's been my retirement plan for a long time. But I couldn't leave Rick."

"I appreciate it. Seriously. And for staying on with me. I was in over my head."

Demming gave him a deep nod. "It's been my pleasure. I wanted to make sure you were settled. It'll always be a little over your head, that's how these places are. You'll learn not to put things off until tomorrow, and you'll keep up all right."

"Yeah. I hear you. So, you'll have to come after I convince this cowgirl to join on and show her the basics, and I'll help you load your Pod."

"I will be happy to show her around. Teach her all the tricks of this place. And I'll leave her with my cell number, just in case. You're going to be lucky to have her, she's got just the right..." Demming looked like he was searching for a word.

"She's a cowboy."

That was what the job was, after all. Cattle, horses, critters, land management—and knowing about kids.

"That's it. She's a hand. I'm looking forward to talking with her again." Demming finished his coffee and stood. "Well. The boss needs me at nine thirty, so I'd best go do my chores."

"Good deal. I'll see you. Holler if you need me out at the barns." He had to wonder why Uncle Rick hadn't made some sort of an office.

"You know I will." Demming patted his shoulder and left out the kitchen door.

He poured another cup of coffee and started bacon in the oven. Bacon and eggs would hold the boys until the doughnuts came.

His timing was good because Jaxson appeared just after he closed the oven, looking sleepy in his PJ top, underwear and pony slippers. "Hi."

"Mornin', you. You want a cup of cocoa?" He knew the answer was yes, so he grabbed Jaxson's favorite mug from the dish drainer.

"Uh-huh. Are you having coffee?" Jaxson sat in one of the kitchen chairs.

"I am. My veins are flowing with coffee." He winked over and started the milk on the stove. "What's on your plan today, son?"

"Gonna swim. Gonna feed the chickens and get eggs, 'cause it's my day. Maybe, if you want, we could ride for a little ways? And then I want to see if Dad will make steaks and potatoes for supper."

"Steaks and potatoes. Steaks and potatoes." Jayden wandered in, singing his brother's words, and went right to the fridge.

"Cocoa, son?"

"Orange juice, thank you. Can we have cherry turnovers for dessert too?" Jayden beamed at him. "I could *murder* a steak."

Jaxson snorted. "Steak is already dead, dummy."

"We don't call names in this house, Jaxson Jericho-Westin," Connor's stern voice came from somewhere on the staircase.

"Sorry, Dad." Jaxson rolled his eyes, then stuck his tongue out at his brother, who made a wonky face back.

"Y'all be good. Dorkfishes." Early poured more coffee and handed over the cocoa.

"Mm. Cocoa." Jaxson blew on it to cool it off.

"I could murder a steak too. Is that the dinner plan? I'll marinate a few." Connor came right to him and kissed him, then they exchanged knowing looks. "Good morning, husband."

"Good morning, my sweetie poopsie boo." Early winked at him and handed him coffee. "Your sons have requested steaks, potatoes, and cherry turnovers. I would like to add a spinach salad, I think."

"And my sons think I'm capable of making cherry

turnovers, honey doodle pop?" Connor winked at him. "I will call Mamaw."

"That's cheating!" Jayden took his juice to the table and sat with Jaxson.

"What are those *names*?" Jaxson sounded disgusted. "Ugh. You guys are so weird."

"We're just in *love*," he teased. "One day, son, this'll be you."

"Nope. I'm going to be too busy for that."

Connor raised an eyebrow. "Doing what?"

"Running the ranch! Duh, Dad."

"Oh. Sure. Duh." Connor leaned on him. "Are you too busy too be in love, Mr. Rancher?"

"Not even a little, Mr. Rancher." He loved this, so much. His family, here. It was still a little dreamlike.

"Gross. Gross. Gross. Are you making bacon?" Jayden sniffed the air.

"I am. I thought bacon and eggs for breakfast before the pool?"

"Yes, please!" the boys said at once.

Connor chuckled. "Are we having our meeting on the deck while the boys swim?" Connor was dressed, but the boys never bothered, they went straight to the pool after breakfast every single day.

"We are. Demming will pull up about nine thirty."

"Oh, good. The whole gang. I like that, because she'll know we're serious." Connor got the eggs out of the fridge and a big bowl to scramble them in. "And Demming can show her around a little more after if she has time."

"That's what I told him. She'll ask clearer questions if I'm not there." Early hoped she was the right person for the job. He had a feeling about her. He'd loved what she said she stood for, that she had a wife to move into the bunkhouse, and they were wanting to start a family.

Ranches needed critters and kids.

"Who, Daddy?" Jaxson asked.

"Daddy's trying to hire a foreman. Demming wants to go live out in California with his daughter and his grandkids, and he's worked hard here. He deserves a break." Connor poured the eggs into the big frying pan.

"Yeah. He says Disney is there and Hollywood too. Me and brother want to go on a Disney cruise one day."

"Let's go on a Carnival one, Jax. One with the big slides." Jayden got points for not calling his brother a baby.

Connor gave him the side eye. "How do these kids know so much about cruises?"

"Blame my mother. She's obsessed." Early shook his head. She was convinced Christmas cruises would be fun. He maintained that he wanted a tree. Presents. Parties. Lights. Sleighrides. The train.

Connor shrugged. "They have all the playground they need here."

"Yep. And I need their help in the quest for perfect ranch lights and a singing big mouth bass in a Santa hat." It would go perfectly in the front room.

Connor shook his head. He expected an emphatic no, but instead he got, "What does he sing?"

"Jingle Bells."

Connor blinked, eyelashes fluttering. "You just—you didn't even hesitate, Early."

"I told you. They're cool."

"I guess this is what being a bazillonaire does for you? Dreams of singing fishes on wooden plaques singing Jingle Bells?" A skillet size portion of scrambled eggs landed on the counter in a big bowl. "Well, if you get that, then I want

Santa and his sleigh and all his reindeer." He grinned at Early. "On the *roof*."

"I will make that happen." He could totally hire it done, but he'd threaten to get up there himself a half dozen times first.

"Awesome." Connor sat plates next to the eggs. "Bacon?"

"We're getting reindeer on the roof!" The boys high-fived.

"No one loves the singing bass like I do," Early lamented as he went for the bacon.

"Awww. I promise to at least try to enjoy the singing fish in a Santa hat." Connor lied so well.

"Thank you." He watched his sons inhale their first breakfast. That was impressive. It was like a weird magic trick where the food went into a black hole, and it didn't seem to do anything.

Connor had taken a small plate for himself and was only half finished when the boys brought their plates to the sink. "Hoovers."

"Bathing suits!" The boys took off at a run.

"Easy on the stairs, boys!" Connor rolled his eyes. "I don't know why I bother saying that."

"That pool was the best idea I've had since the boys. They love it." Early shook his head. If he didn't have an interview, he'd jump in himself.

"Are you sure the boys were your idea?" Connor winked at him. They had been and they both knew it. Not the adopting kids part but adopting these particular kids part.

"Pretty sure, but we both fell in love, so that didn't matter." They'd been so little—scared and skinny and desperate for connection and attention. They had all needed each other.

"How could we not?" Connor took the dishes to the sink

and started loading up the dishwasher. "Thanks for the bacon. I'll get this cleaned up. Do you want to find us a nice spot by the pool for this meeting?"

"I'm on it." Early patted Connor's butt on the way by.

"Easy, cowboy, I'm a little tender there today." Connor clearly wasn't complaining; he sounded pleased about that.

"I'll get you a cushion for your chair outside." It was going to be a great interview.

21

Reese brought the doughnuts from the best doughnut shop in fifty miles so as far as the kids were concerned, she was hired. They weren't taking into consideration whether Reese actually intended to accept the position, but kids were great judges of character and Connor had to agree, it was hers if she wanted it.

She and Early started off talking shop though, and he was trying to follow, but he had to admit there was a lot he just didn't understand. So he sipped his coffee and munched on his Boston cream doughnut while he listened.

"—raise cattle for meat or did you want to start a breeding program?"

"I'm thinking about Simmentals. There are some amazing Charolais ranches here already, so...let's try something new." Early must have said something interesting, because Reese leaned in.

"Simmentals have trouble calving sometimes. What's your thought on crossing them with Beefmasters? They'll calve easier, they're bigger, but you'll still have nice, lean meat..."

Listen to them saying all those words that made so little sense.

But there was no doubt she was taking the job. She and Early got along so well, like they'd known each other forever. Maybe he didn't need to understand it all right now. He understood enough to know they were talking about investing some money, though.

"Can I interrupt to ask a totally non-cowboy talk question, that's way less fun than this conversation?" He set his coffee down.

Reese glanced at Early, then grinned at him. "You're the one with the budget, huh?"

"Not yet. There literally is no budget. I haven't found a laptop or a ledger or anything, and Demming says whatever he needed he just asked Rick for."

"Okay. So how can I help? Seriously—I can get stats for you, feed costs, all of it. That's what y'all are hiring me for. I'm not looking to punch cattle for a living. I want to be a bad-assed foreman for a big set-up. I want to be a part of a legacy." There was passion in Reese's voice, a ferocity in her eyes. "There's a home here, and you said that if Dana has babies, you're good with it."

"I am. This is going to be a family place." Early nodded, matching her energy.

"So yes, we want this to be a family ranch, a fun place for the kids to grow up. We definitely want it to be home. But Early also wants to make it profitable and that's where I come in. Stats and costs are exactly what I need. I think Demming might be helpful there. But I also need to value the ranch. How many animals, what they're worth, how close to capacity are we? How much more help do we need?"

He was going to work on the property value too.

Insurance. Investments. Those things were squarely in his wheelhouse. "We need to know where we are now before we can grow."

"Totally. I know that the mustang program is a serious labor of love and gets us that BLM land, but you have to be able to weather the bad years. A breeding program will help out, but you need to cull and sell anyone that's not producing."

Okay, that made sense. He mostly followed all of that. "So listen. I know nothing. I didn't follow a word of that conversation you two were having, I was brought up in the suburbs... I'm going to learn, but I have to ask for some patience. And there are going to be tons of things I just don't know we need. Early's not going anywhere, but—tell me if I'm wrong, honey—I think he wants to get his hands dirty and not have to worry about this part." That wasn't a dig, Early was so good with the animals and he thought his husband really loved it.

Early nodded, expression serious. "I do. I love this, and I have a degree in water management and quality, so I'm going to spend some serious time assuring that my waterways are healthy, safe places."

He smiled at Early, feeling proud, but also a little guilty for keeping this amazing man cooped up in Denver all these years. He really hadn't understood. But he got it now, and he was all in for Early, and for their family. It wasn't too late at all.

"Dude, you know how much that rocks? I want to learn about that too. Once we get the budget parts buttoned up, of course." Reese grinned at him. "Can I start today?"

He was so relieved for Early. This had been a long process and he'd really wanted Reese on board. It was great to see it happening. "If we're agreed on the salary, I think we're good here."

"I talked to Dana last night. She's interviewing with the school today, and she's in. All the way."

"I'm looking forward to meeting her. Imagine if she ends up teaching our boys?" He chuckled. "Do you and Dana have plans tonight? We'd love to have you join us for dinner. I'm grilling steaks."

"Ooh...steaks? Lucky." Demming walked up, all grins, and Early snorted like a fractious horse.

"Like there's ever—ever—been a supper your happy backside wasn't invited to."

Demming's laugh filled the air. "I've got plans. I'm actually going to your folks' for supper. Your Momma's making that pasta salad with chicken, and we're going to play cards."

"Oh, lucky you. You're having cherry turnovers for dessert." He knew because he'd called and asked if Momma would make them for the kids. "Reese, have you met Demming Rogers?"

"I know of him, yessir. I used to watch you rope on the Mountain States circuit when I was up visiting in Greeley with my granddaddy." Reese stood and held out one scarred-up hand.

Cowboys were all the same, Connor guessed. Scars were stories, the land was important, and respect was everything.

"You're really reaching through the cobwebs there." Demming shook. "Pleased. I've heard good things."

"Excellent. I'm ready to learn everything you got time to teach me."

Demming grinned. "I take it you got yourself a job?"

"Yessir, I do." Reese didn't even hesitate.

"The bad news is with her living on property she won't

be bringing doughnuts every morning." He laughed but he was watching Early who looked relieved and happy. That was a look he could get used to.

"Get one of the guys to buy them on his way in, Early." Demming rolled his eyes. "Bosses."

"Ha!" He would never be the boss. That was Early's job. "Those are the bosses, over there in the pool. I just work here."

"Jayden and Jaxson, right? How old are they?" Reese asked him. "They're little fishes, aren't they?"

"They're six and ten. Early created a monster when he put in this pool."

"I'd have put them closer together."

"Jaxson is a very big six, and Jayden is a young, smaller ten." Early winked at Reese and pulled a face. "Although, let me tell you, they can discover trouble. No sweat."

"They take after Early that way."

Demming laughed out loud. "That's the truth."

Early rolled his eyes and shrugged. "What do you want me to say? I'm an overachiever."

"Well, you ready to get to work?" Demming grinned at Reese. "Because I'm ready to retire."

"Yessir! Let me text my wife, and you can take me on the rounds." She glanced at Early. "Watch that little jackass Ian, boss. He's a creeper."

"Yeah, thanks. He's not allowed on the property. I still can't believe him."

Connor growled under his breath at Ian's name. He wanted the bastard far away from his family—his kids and Early.

Reese nodded to him, pushed back her chair, and pulled out her phone. "Yeah. That's how I'd be. Be right with you, Demming."

"I like her," Demming said, and Early's lips pursed.

"I do too. This might work."

He rolled his eyes. "This *will* work. And I'm not being optimistic. She's great."

"Dad! Watch!" Jaxson cannonballed into the pool, water splashing everywhere.

"Oh lord." He shook his head. "Five more minutes and then you have to do chicken things!" He was pretty sure it was Jaxson's day.

"Wet butts make chicken feathers stick!" Jaxson squealed and mooned them.

"He's not wrong," Demming offered without cracking a smile.

"That's your fault," he pinned Early with a teasing look.

"Well, he does have his facts right." Butter wouldn't melt in Early's mouth.

"The two of you." Connor laughed and rolled his eyes. "I need to go inside to put a couple more steaks in the marinade and make a dressing for the spinach salad someone requested." He gave Early a quick kiss. "Stay out of trouble. Send the boys in when you're done here."

"Will do, darlin'. Come on, boys! Time for chores, then you can screw off until lunch."

"Daddy said screw!" Jaxson hollered, and Jayden rolled his eyes.

"Screw isn't a bad word. You screw in a...a...a screw."

Demming snorted. "Logical."

"Jayden is often too smart for his own good. He considers it a challenge." Early smiled happily. "So do I."

Demming winked. "Good luck with that one. Reese is giving me a wave. I'll report back." Demming waved at Reese and headed down the steps from the pool deck.

"Lord have mercy." Early took his hand for a second. "You happy with this?"

"I have been happy since I got here. But yes. I'm happy with this. I know you are; I can see it in your eyes."

"I am. I'm thinking this is a new beginning." Early was... glowing.

"I'm thinking I have never been more in love with you than I am right now." Connor had a lot to work out still, but he definitely had a job to do. It wasn't lawyering, which he still wanted to fit in somehow, but it was going to keep him plenty busy until they had this place rolling.

He pulled Early in close. "I get to kiss you at work. What's better than that?"

"I got nothing, darlin'. Not a thing." His husband took a deep breath and let it out. "Did I tell you I got you a purse dog?"

He laughed. "A what?"

"Two lab puppies for the boys and a Shih Tzu for you. Little, fuzzy—it'll be perfect."

He was still giggling. A Shih Tzu. How fucking adorable. "I better be careful, something on the ranch might eat him. Did you get me a purse too? Oh, he can ride on my Harley!"

"Goggles, little leather vest and cap..." Early was onboard.

"Stop that." God, this man could make him laugh. A Shih Tzu. Well, he'd teach it to growl at people he didn't like.

"A pretty little puppy with fuzzy ears and lots of wiggles." Early hooked arms with him. "They'll be here this afternoon."

"What? Today? Do we have food? Kennels? Dog beds? Things to chew on? Do the kids know? I better get the house ready."

Early blinked at him. "Yes. No. No. No. No. No, and okay."

"Stop that too." He glared at his husband. They weren't ready for one puppy much less three. "I need to go shopping."

The boys appeared wrapped in towels. "Are there more doughnuts?"

"No more doughnuts."

"Chickens," Early pointed.

"They're best fried," Jayden shot back.

Early snorted. "Eggs. Chickens. Feeding. Now."

He watched them go. Early was so good at that. The boys always pushed him a little harder. "What's on your chore list while I'm getting D.O.G. things?"

"Getting Reese up to date, getting you all the paperwork for the finances that I have, cleaning the hot tub, normal stuff."

"Normal stuff." Connor chuckled. He didn't have a normal yet, but he would. Or maybe not. Maybe this was his normal now, wrangling kids, running errands. Maybe normal was a day-to-day thing now. Maybe that wasn't such a bad situation. "Go on. I love you. I'll be back with stuff before lunch. There's chicken salad."

"I love you, darlin'." Early went to get another cup of coffee, waving at him.

22

All of Reese's paperwork was done, Demming's move-out date arranged, the ladies' move-in date set. Early had called his dad, done some work, fed and corralled kids, and made them get out and currycomb horses until they were pooped.

Now Connor was home, with his new Range Rover filled to the brim with god knew what, the dogs were on the way, and Early was...well, he was wanting a beer and a steak.

Lord, he was a spoiled man.

Connor climbed the porch steps. "Hey, you. Help me unpack? There's dog beds and crates in the back of the car. I've got bowls and chewy toys and stuff here." Connor rattled a big bag he was carrying.

"I will. The boys are in the pool again." Early chuckled and shook his head, tickled as shit. Connor was so excited about the dogs, and that suited him to the bone. "They are going to sleep tonight. They brushed all the riding horses for their afternoon chores."

"You're not fooling around. I love how they just crash every night now." Connor put the bag down and headed back to the Range Rover. "I did my homework. The Labs are going to need bigger crates eventually, but the guys at the store said these were good for a while. And the smaller one is for Sophie."

"Sophie?" Oh, so cute! He loved it. "That's adorable. They're about ten minutes out. Do you think Frick and Frack out there would be pleased?"

"Sophie if it's a girl. If it's a boy I'm going with Ollie. And Frick and Frack are going to love this." Connor winked at him and hauled two of the dog beds up onto the porch.

They managed to get the SUV unloaded right as a pickup truck trundled up the road.

"That's them. Should I get the boys or let them...discover our new family members."

"Well, why don't we let the pups sniff around a little and then get them? So they're less overwhelmed by all the squealing and snuggling." Connor chuckled.

"Good idea. Come on. Let's do this." Early led Connor over to the truck.

A young lady climbed out of the passenger side, a little white and gray ball of fluff in her arms. "Hey, y'all. She's really scared. The big pups are barking like crazy. Can someone help Momma or take her, or both?"

"Oh, I think she must be mine. I've got her." Connor stepped right up and took the little fluffball, holding her to his chest. He was so protective, it was adorable. "Hey, little girl. I'll get her settled in a crate in a quiet place and come right back to help."

Early went and helped a dark brown and a golden pup down, both of them wiggling and barking and peeing.

"Meet Goldie and Brownie. Two girls. Both fixed. Both thirteen weeks old. Both convinced that everyone loves them to death."

"Goldie and Brownie. I'm Early."

"Martha, and this is my daughter Heidi and..."

"DADDY!" Jaxson's scream split the air and two wet, mostly naked, excited boys came tumbling down the stairs.

"Boys," he snapped. "Gentle. Do not scare them."

They both skidded to a halt a few feet away. "Sorry, Daddy."

"They're so cute though." Jaxson was wiggling where he stood he was so excited.

"This is Brownie and Goldie. They're puppies, and this is a brand-new place, with brand-new people. Jayden, you remember that a little, right? Coming home to us?"

"Yes, sir. I was *worried*."

"Are they worried?" Jaxson asked quietly.

"A little, but they're also wanting to meet you both. You're going to be their people."

"Can we pet them?"

"Yes, but be easy." Early glanced at Martha. "Would y'all like to come up to the kitchen?"

"That would be nice, thank you."

Heidi looked at the two boys. "We can bring them up, and then I can show you how they like to play. Okay?"

"Okay." Jayden was very serious all of a sudden. "We want to take good care of them."

"Don't worry," Heidi smiled at him. "They're going to love you guys."

Jaxson glanced up at him, tears flooding his eyes. "You got us dogs."

"Y'all have proven that you'll work for it, son." He opened his arms. "Need a hug?"

Jaxson ran right over, sniffling. "They're so cute."

"They are. And y'all are going to have fun teaching them things." He held on tight, picking Jaxson up and leading the way to the kitchen. "Find out what folks want to drink, Jayden?"

The kitchen was packed with doggie stuff, and the pups went right for the toys.

Jayden took drink orders and Connor met him in the kitchen, helping to pour iced tea and lemonade. "Sophie's in her crate around the corner, I'm just letting her chill for a few minutes while the big dogs are settling down."

"Sophie is a good name, Dad." Jayden sounded so confident.

Jaxson frowned. "Who's Sophie?"

"Dad's dog." Again, that confidence.

"How did you know Dad had a dog?" That pout was getting bigger by the second, and Early was going to have to put Jaxson down for a nap.

"I just listened, Jax." Jayden shrugged. "Can we play with the puppies now, Daddy? Which one is mine?"

"Y'all should spend some time with them, now. See what happens." One would gravitate to one boy, and the other would need her own attention.

"Come on, Jax." Jayden took Jax's hand when Early set him down and they went to pet the puppies.

Connor handed out drinks. "They're adorable. Do you breed? Are they rescues? This was all a big surprise to me."

"They're all rescues. We foster constantly. We also have two middle-aged mixes and a Saint Bernard, so this is a huge help." Martha murmured her thanks for the iced tea. "Now I can get more babies from the rescue and socialize them."

"You're doing a good thing." Connor's eyes were on the boys. "And my boys are happy, so that's a win."

"We all have our calling, that's for sure."

Jayden had the chocolate lab in his lap, and Jaxson was playing tug with the yellow.

Connor pulled out his phone. "Can you give me the name of the rescue? We'll make a donation. Don't you think, Early?"

"Absolutely. We'll pay the adoption fee, plus a donation, just to help with costs." Early needed to get some of the guys to put up a dog run so they could just let the dogs out to potty. He sent Demming a text to have it happen.

On it.

Demming's texts were always like that. One word, maybe two.

"Oh." They were interrupted by a tiny little whining from the other room. "Coming Sophie!" Connor jogged off.

"He's already in love," Martha muttered.

"She's going to be sleeping in our bed, I know it." The man deserved a puppy. He'd never seen anyone who needed one more.

"What about you?" Martha asked slyly. "You need a dog, don't you? What are you looking for?"

"I have two Labs here, plus a half dozen ranch dogs. When the right one shows up, I'll know."

Martha chuckled. "I see how you are. I'll keep my eyes open."

"She jumped right into my arms when I opened the crate." Connor came back with a bundle of fluff in his arms. "Look, honey."

"Oh, look at you. You're a dollbaby, aren't you?"

She looked right at him and barked, like she was getting it said.

Everyone laughed. "She's going to rule this house in a

week." Heidi shook her head. "Those little ones never understand how little they are."

"Daddy! This one's peeing!" Jaxson pointed to the little pup.

"Outside with them, tell them to potty outside, and tell them they're good when they do. Use a leash. Go."

"Heidi, follow along and help, baby? Show them what to do?"

"Heidi, there are leashes..." Connor pointed to a pile of brand-new leashes on the kitchen counter.

"Got it!" She grabbed two and ran after the boys.

Connor grabbed a paper towel and some urine-b-gone type spray. Thank god they didn't have carpet.

"Here." He got a fluffy puppy as Connor went to clean up. "I have pee pads if we need them, but mostly I guess they can be outside. The boys usually are." Connor was surprisingly not stressed. If this had happened in their place in Denver, Connor would have pitched a fit. That was one of the reasons they didn't have pets in Denver.

"I'm having a dog run put in, so that'll be easier." Early scratched fluffball under the chin.

"Oh, that's a good idea. Wow that's a lot of pee for a little guy." Connor tossed the paper towels and washed his hands. "Thanks for sending your daughter out to help."

Martha smiled. "She's good with kids."

"And dogs," Early added, earning himself a laugh.

"They are, basically, the same thing."

Connor took Sophie back and unwrapped a matching pink camouflage collar and leash. "Hey, little girl. You should probably go outside too for a bit, huh?"

Pink camo. That was adorable. Early couldn't be more in love.

"How cute. I'd have pegged him for a big dog kind of

guy." Martha watched Connor go. "Listen, I hate to do this, but I have to ask you something."

Early nodded, frowning slightly. That sounded more serious than just puppies. "Sure."

"So... I hesitated to bring them out today, honestly. I'd heard some things in town that concerned me, but other people speak so highly of you... I decided to go with my gut and hope that I'm not making a mistake."

"Concerned you?" What the fuck? What the *actual* fuck? Early forced himself to not get all defensive. "Like what? Demming will vouch for me and mine."

"I know. A lot of folks did, but..." Martha shrugged. "There's a rumor about how you treat your animals."

Early saw red, and one of his hands clenched into a fist. What? Him? That was ridiculous. "Martha, I'll let you go right now to see my barns, the herds. You can talk to Dr. Maslin or anyone in her practice. I've never hurt an animal in my life."

She reached out and patted his arm. "Look, I'm here, aren't I? I didn't really believe it, but I'd be remiss if I left the dogs here and didn't bring it up. And anyway, I thought you should know."

"Do you know who? Or who you heard it from, so I can weed this out?"

"I don't know. I was in the post office and a couple of guys were talking about it. Uh...youngish shorter guy with sandy hair, a taller skinny guy in a cowboy hat, oh and Percy Albertson, you know him? He runs the big feed store down the way."

"Percy, huh. Okay. I'll go chat with him." He was going to kill someone. "I don't know why someone would spread lies. It ain't right."

"I'm sorry, Early. I hope I didn't insult you." Martha

shrugged, heading for the door. "I'm sure you understand I had to bring it up."

"Hey, I appreciate it. Very much. I can't tell folks what the truth is if I have no idea someone's being evil." Early found her a warm smile, leaning in and shaking his head. "I've got little boys. I want them to know their daddy is an honest man."

"You keep those puppies happy, and I'll vouch." She gave him a wink. "I'd never heard a bad thing about Rick either."

"I'll keep the puppies healthy and happy." He wasn't an asshole, not a bit.

"I know. Thank you, Early." Martha stepped out onto the porch. "I'm going to keep my eye out for something I think you might like."

The boys were running in the yard with the puppies, and Connor's little ball of fur was sniffing around on the end of the pink leash.

He loved the smiles on all his guys' faces. All three of them were beaming, love pouring from them.

"Heidi, honey. Time to go."

"Okay." Heidi checked that the boys had a good hold on their leashes and then said something to Connor before jogging over. "It was nice to meet you," she said, offering him a smile.

"I was great to meet both of you. Y'all are welcome to stop in, anytime." And they'd never find a thing to complain about, godammit. He was going to call his daddy and figure this shit out.

Connor hung out with the boys while they pulled out of the driveway, then scooped up Sophie and joined him on the porch. "Okay, I thought I was a big dog person, but she is so cute. Thank you, honey." Connor took a quick kiss but pulled back, smile fading. "What's the matter?"

"Nothing. I got to make a couple of phone calls." He was going to explode, he was so pissed.

Connor's eyes narrowed. "All right. Go make them. But you're going to tell me later."

"Yes. You know I will. You got to help the boys with the dogs. We'll talk in a bit."

Early meant it too, but right now he was calling his folks and having ears put to the ground.

23

Connor had spent all afternoon with the boys and their puppies, playing, walking, and even a little dozing in the sunshine. He was completely smitten with Sophie—she was just the sweetest little ball of unconditional love he'd ever seen.

He'd finally insisted they put the puppies in their crates and send the boys off for a nap. Jayden was really too old for naps, but he'd start out reading and fall asleep anyway. He always did. The fresh air and all the activity wore him out too.

He hadn't seen or heard a thing from Early all afternoon, and he knew something was wrong. Early had been wound up tight after Martha and Heidi left. He respected that his husband hadn't wanted to talk about it then, there was too much going on, but Connor decided to find him now. Hopefully whatever it was had been resolved.

But Early didn't have an office, so where would he go to make phone calls? This house was so damn big.

They needed an office. A real office with desks and supplies. It was important.

He'd talk to Early, assuming he could find the man...

He searched everywhere, finally finding the door to the secret room open. Bingo.

He knocked softly on the pocket door jamb before climbing the stairs to the round library. "Coming up."

"I'm up here, darlin'. You need help with the dogs?" Early sounded absolutely livid.

"No, they're crashed in their crates, and the kids are having a nap before company comes." He didn't remember ever seeing Early so angry...and it had been hours too. He moved into the room slowly. "You've been up here a while?"

"I have. We got a problem. I don't know what to do about it. I need help."

Well, okay then.

He nodded and pulled over a chair. He tried not to worry, but Early didn't ask often, so he knew this was serious. "Okay. I'm listening."

"Someone's been spreading rumors—that I'm an animal abuser, a child abuser, that I have been unfaithful to you. It's not good. Martha let me know."

He stared at Early, squinting like that might make things clearer. "What? I don't...what?" It was ridiculous. No one who knew Early would believe it.

"I know! She almost didn't consider us for the dogs." Early was shaking. Literally shaking.

"Hey. We got them. So, she knows it's bullshit, and half this town won't believe it either." Connor stood and moved around behind Early's chair to massage his shoulders. "God, you're wound up tight. Take a breath."

"I called Pop, and he ran down to the feed store to chat with the folks there. Someone's saying we abuse our boys."

He froze, lifting his hands carefully from Early's shoulders.

He hit on the someone quickly. It wasn't much of a puzzle. "Maybe the same someone that told Reese you hired him for the job?" He paced away from Early. He should be keeping it together since Early was already losing it but...abuse the boys? "I'll kill him. Abuse our boys. I dare anyone to try to prove that."

"Can we do something? I mean, being a bitch isn't illegal, is it? I have a baseball bat." Early had a gun too, but his husband didn't threaten to use it.

"Yeah. If we can find out for sure who it was, then yeah. We just need to know, and to be able to prove it. After that, I'm a lawyer, I can do something about almost anything." Anything said against them had an effect on their business and their bottom line, that was defamation. That, he could fight with legal fire.

"Okay. I bet Pop can help there, a lot. He knows everybody, and who he doesn't know, Momma does." Early glanced at him, then shook his head. "I can't believe this shit..."

"I don't understand it. Why mess with our kids? Our livelihood? I'm getting a fucking restraining order if we can prove this. I'll talk to Pop in the morning." He paced back to Early and sat, taking his husband's hands. "Listen. This is bullshit, and I'm not going to let it stand. But you need to breathe, you're all red-faced and wound up. You're going to blow a gasket."

"I don't want to do that. I just want to live without this little fucker bothering us. I didn't lead him on, Connor. I swear to god!"

He squeezed Early's fingers. "I know." He made sure his words were impossible to misunderstand. "I know. And I trust you." Early was attractive to other people, and why shouldn't he be? But he could be jealous, and he knew that.

It was never about his trust in Early though. It was about getting the other guy to back off his man.

"I just...I hate when something happens like this, and I honestly didn't do anything wrong. It pisses me off."

"My cowboy has a strong sense of justice." He sighed. "I'm pissed too. But I can't imagine anyone that knows you would believe any of this nonsense. If I get a call from the school, or the cops come by, then you'll see some outrage."

"Yeah. Yeah, we get a call from the school, I'm going to... whatever I have to. This is harassment."

"It is. You want to go chop something or build something or shoot at some targets you go ahead. But then we have to be coolheaded. If it is him, he wants us mad. We have to be smarter." He should probably take some of his own advice.

"That's why I'm up here instead of out in my truck. I figured I'd be the better man."

And Connor understood how tough it was for Early to not just fly off the handle.

"I know, honey." He slid into Early's lap and hugged him. "You're always the better man."

"Liar. I try, though. I want the boys to grow up and be like you."

Early's words hit him like an arrow to the heart. His lover knew how to make him proud.

"They'll get the best of both of us." He took a kiss, because he wanted to Early to know how proud he was of his family. Early included. "We'll get through this, and we'll be stronger and smarter for it. You'll see."

"We'll get through it, and we'll run someone out of town on a goddamn rail," Early grumbled, proving that temper was right under the surface.

"And that too. For good." He climbed off Early's lap. "I love you, cowboy. I'm going to go downstairs to start your spinach salad and meet Momma, because she's dropping off dessert. Take your time, but when you come down, please be ready for guests, boys, and puppies."

"I'll come down. Fuming up here isn't going to help, and I want to meet all the puppies." Early hauled himself up and took his hand. "Tell me how much you love your Sophie."

"Oh my god, Early, she is such a little fuzzball of love. She's so tiny! I adore her." He started down the stairs, Early's laughter chasing him.

"You'll be taking her everywhere, now. I know it."

"Once she stops peeing every time I pick her up, yes. I will. And she can sleep in my lap while I work at the desk I don't have in the office we desperately need." He chuckled. That was subtle as an anvil.

"Yeah, I figured you could plan that. I want to make sure that we can see the pool, make sure there aren't any bears in it."

"Bears." He rolled his eyes. "I'll plan it, but the bears won't go near the pool with the boys always in it." He could make them a nice office. What room had a good view of the pool though? Other than theirs? He'd have to think about that.

"Bears. Although apparently, we put stock tanks out for them so they aren't interested."

"Wait. We really have bears?" Connor peered out the window like he'd be able to see them right now.

"We do. A Momma brown bear and cubs. We keep them as far away from the house as possible."

"I hope so. Do the boys know what to do about a bear?" Did he? He wasn't sure.

"Well, if they're out before I go check the chemicals and clean, they're in big trouble, but I've told them to avoid Mama bear, especially in the spring."

"We better watch the puppies too." When they got to the kitchen, there was a little covered basket on the counter. "Looks like Momma dropped by, and we missed her." Not that she would have found them up in that room.

Three puppies had fresh puppy pads, a new toy, and a little blanket of their own, obviously from their new granny. Early looked it all over and shook his head.

"Good lord and butter."

"And dessert. She's the best. Let's get you chopping things for the salad. That'll keep you busy." He pulled out the spinach, and a bunch of veggies, some hard-boiled eggs, tomatoes… whatever he could find. He was a fan of salads full of stuff.

"Daddy, can I help?" Jayden came wandering out, half-smiling, half-scowling.

"Of course. Wash your hands. I'll get you to help with the eggs. We're having Reese and her wife up for supper." Early always acted like the boys were welcome in the kitchen.

"Are those the dog ladies?"

"Nope. You know how Demming is moving to California? Reese is going to be the foreman, and her wife is coming to live in the house. She's a schoolteacher."

"Does she teach at our new school?" Jayden washed up but dried his hands off on his T-shirt.

"We have towels," he reminded his son with a sigh.

Jayden rolled his eyes.

"She's interviewing there."

"Is she pretty?"

Early shrugged. "I guess we'll find out this evening. You'll have to tell me."

Jayden nodded. "I totally will. I know your cuteometer is a little screwy."

He snorted a laugh. "Aren't you a little young to judge someone's cuteometer?"

Jayden crossed his arms. "Nooo. Jennifer Hugh wanted to be my girlfriend."

"Redhead Jennifer?"

"Uh-huh."

"You're kind of young for a girlfriend." Way too young. His boys could date when they were thirty.

"Da-a-ad! I said she wanted to. I didn't say yes."

Early's lips twitched. "What did you say, son?"

"Ask me when school started. I want to see the other girls."

He knew he shouldn't do it, but he couldn't stop himself. He laughed out loud and leaned against Early. "Gotta keep those options open."

"That's my boy. You never know what you want until you see what's there."

"Right? I mean, what if I'm Jennifer's boyfriend and I find a girl who likes to swim more? Or who's better at math and can help me with my homework?"

Connor was going to die.

Jayden looked at Early perfectly seriously. "So, you needed help with the eggs?"

"I totally did. Are you comfortable with trying to peel? They don't have to be perfect." How did Early do that? Just be straight-faced like Jayden wasn't the funniest kid on earth.

"I can do it, I bet." Jayden picked one up and tapped it on the counter.

Connor just kept on giggling as he washed the spinach, hoping the running water would cover the sound. He didn't have Early's self-control.

"So, did I like to...*swim* more?" Early whispered to him, teasing wildly.

"No, you liked to fuck more," he whispered back, not helping his case of giggles at all.

"Boy howdy." He got a wink, a happy chuckle, and then Jaxson was there.

"The puppies need to go out. I need help."

"I'm coming, son." Early took out Sophie and one of the Labs, Jaxson took out the other.

He watched them leave because Sophie on a leash was too cute, like taking a dust bunny for a walk.

"So...you really like it here, huh?" Jayden asked peeling an egg and not looking at him.

"I told you I would." He set the spinach on the counter and ruffled Jayden's hair. "Are you ready for school to start?"

"Yeah. We've already got friends, and soon it'll be too cold to swim all the time here. Do you think it'll be different?"

"School? Maybe. I think there are fewer kids than back in Denver, but the school itself is bigger. But like you said, you already have a few friends, so you know you'll meet more."

Jayden nodded, working the shell off the egg like he was defusing a bomb. "Yeah, and everyone wants to know us. That's cool too. Are you going to help Daddy run the ranch so that you can come to stuff with us after school?"

"I am. Won't that be great? I don't have to work regular hours anymore, so I can come to everything." He wasn't going to miss anything. "That's one of the best things about running our own business."

"I think it's great. You're going to have so much fun, too. We like the idea of having hang-out afternoons with you too."

"You do, huh? Then I guess this whole ranch thing is good for us." When did Jayden get so grown up? He sounded like a teenager already. "Are you excited about your puppy?"

"Duh! I love her! She's so pretty, and I'm going to teach her how to catch a ball and swim and bite bad guys and lead the blind!"

Lead the blind. He managed not to laugh this time. "Ambitious. What if she just wants to play and snuggle?"

"Daddy says ranch dogs need jobs. Is that a good enough job to keep her?"

Oh, so sweet. "Yes. That's a good enough job for any dog. But if Daddy says you should keep her busy, there's plenty for her to learn."

"First, don't poop in the house."

"Yes." He grinned at his son. "Or pee. Or chew on anything but chew toys, especially not Sophie."

"Brownie's going to be the best dog, Dad. You may have to watch out for Goldie." That wink was pure wickedness. "She did pick Jaxson..."

"You are very observant, buddy." Jaxson and Jayden were not their biological children, but it didn't matter. Jayden took after him, and Jaxson was just like his Daddy.

"Hopefully, they will wear each other out enough they can only get into so much trouble."

"Can they swim? What if they jump in the pool? What are you going to do when we're at school?"

"I think Labs swim pretty well. And we will look after them. They're yours mostly, but they're family dogs. Don't worry."

"Daddy promised that there will be a running yard thing for them, and once a week we have to pick the poop up. Do you too, since you got a dog?"

"Hm. I don't know. Since Daddy and I are buying all the groceries I think maybe you boys can do some chores for us." He winked.

"Yeah. Outside chores are cooler than inside ones. Inside chores suck." Jayden shot him another look. "Daddy fired Ian, and he was cleaning the house and stuff. Ian was *mad.*"

"Oh?" It was hard to school his expression and stay cool, but he managed it. "Did Ian say something to you?"

"Yeah, but it's not nice." Jayden sort of glanced away from him. He knew that look. He'd known it since Jayden was barely able to make himself understood.

It infuriated him, that Ian would say something around his kids that they didn't even feel like they could repeat. He was angry under the surface, but he kept his lawyer face on for his son. "Sometimes when a grown-up asks, it's okay to say not nice things. You can tell me, it's okay."

"He said that Daddy fired him because you found out they were in love. I told him that you were married and kiss all the time." Jayden shook his head. "I know I'm a kid, but Daddy talks about you all the time. Daddy never talked about him. Never."

He couldn't answer right away; there was too much in what Jayden just said to unpack gracefully. He took a breath, then nodded. "Daddy and I are solid as a rock. You told him the right thing." He took another breath. "Hey, can you do me a favor, and run out and see if Daddy needs help with Sophie? Two puppies is a lot." He could hold it together another thirty seconds.

"Okay! Watch my eggs?" Jayden grinned at him. "Brownie! Brownie, I'm coming!"

He gripped the counter with both hands, willing the marble to crumble under his fingers. In *love*? Ian dared... *dared* to say that to his children? "I'm getting a fucking restraining order," he said out loud, making it more real. And if he saw that face again, he wasn't even going to think about it, he was going give Ian a taste of his fist.

Early was out there, laughing at the boys, at the dogs. There was no way that his husband was in love with anyone else.

He paced the kitchen and made the salad, trying to cool off before their guests arrived.

Early came in with Sophie. "I locked the boys and their dogs on the deck. They'll be safe there."

He nodded. "Good idea." He didn't know what to say about Ian, so he said nothing. Early wasn't at fault; he didn't doubt his husband at all, but he knew Early worried about that, and he didn't want to add any fuel to that fire. He found a smile for Early instead. "The salad is done. Have a look at your mother's turnover's they're gorgeous."

"I'll put the potatoes in the oven, and that just leaves the steaks." Early was whistling softly, putting Sophie down on the kitchen floor.

"I'll go start up the grill so it will be ready when Reese and her wife come." He stopped as he was about to leave the kitchen. "Early, I think we have to warn Reese about Ian. Tell her what's going on. We don't want her blindsided in town or..." He sighed. "Maybe she won't want to deal with this circus."

"Maybe she won't, but I bet she will." Early had that look on his face—tight around the eyes, but still smiling—that meant trouble. "Regardless, we're going to fix it. Straight up."

"Damn right." He went out to the grill to get it going. He could hear the boys playing, the puppies yipping and having fun. It was important to him that their boys didn't get caught up in any of this and he'd do whatever he needed to make sure they were insulated from it.

Hopefully Reese was of the same mindset.

Speak of the devil, Reese pulled up with a passenger, parking her pickup next to Early's. She hopped out, waved, and then grabbed a plate from the console as her wife left the truck too.

"We brought cheese and veggies to share," she called.

He waved back and took a breath, which was somehow easier with Reese here. She was part of their future, part of the ranch's future. Smiling was easier too, and he jogged over to take the plate and shake hands. "Hello. Welcome, welcome. You must be Dana."

"I am! You must be Connor." Dana was pretty and blonde, and she had a kind smile.

"Yes. Please, come in. The boys are playing with their new puppies." Which obviously was better than the swimming pool right now. "Hey, honey. Reese and Dana are here," he called through the screen door before opening it.

"—SWEAR to god, I thought that steer was going to leap over the trailer like Evel Knievel, and Reese was standing there, just staring like she was hypnotized." Dana winked, and they all cracked up.

All except Jayden.

Jayden stared at Reese's wife like she'd hung the moon or held the ladder for the guy who'd done it.

Early had never seen anything like it.

"I guess it turned out all right, you're both sitting here." Connor was still chuckling. "Did the trailer make it?"

The ladies glanced at each other, then they grinned. "Mostly."

Connor laughed. "That would definitely come out of your paycheck."

"Are you going to live here now? Do you like dogs? We got puppies. Are you going to have a dog? Do you like kids too? Because I'm a kid." Jaxson took a big breath. He must have been holding onto those questions for a while.

Dana smiled at Jaxson, then at Jayden, who blushed almost purple. "We are! We love dogs. We have a little cocker spaniel named Molly. I love your puppies, and I like children a lot! I'm a kindergarten teacher."

"I finished kindergarten." Jaxson nodded. "I liked it. You'll be a good teacher, I bet."

It was all Early could do not to laugh as Jayden caught Connor looking at him and stuffed a forkful of salad in his mouth.

They chatted for a few more minutes, and then the boys asked permission to get in the pool, which worked, because they needed to talk about the rumors floating around. They set up with wine glasses and candles out by the pool to keep an eye out, and Connor glanced at him before sighing and turning to Reese. "So... I have to ask, have you heard anything more from Ian?"

"No, but Demming said that he's been spreading lies."

Early blinked, not sure what to think, but Reese continued.

"Your dad called Demming while we were going over the feed inventory. He's livid." She shook her head. "I swear, that kid is stupid. Demming's going to have his head, if your dad doesn't."

"Apparently it's everything from how we treat our animals to how we treat our children. And livid doesn't really touch where Early and I are at right now." Early watched Connor force himself to relax; he wasn't sure he'd ever seen Connor have to do that before. "What I need is proof that it's Ian...exactly what he said and to whom. Then I can take the legal route so none of us gets charged with assault." Connor seemed to be joking...but also not.

Early agreed wholeheartedly. "I'm not going to have folks believe I'm mean to critters or my sons."

Or any other children that they brought into the family.

"Okay. We'll keep our ears open. I've seen how you treat your animals—with respect, like you treat everyone else."

Dana nodded. "Reese was so upset when she thought she'd lost this opportunity."

Reese rolled her eyes and grinned. "I felt like I belonged here."

"So did I. This is supposed to be a magical place, a good home, and stewardship of the land is important." He believed that this could become a place that people spoke of with respect, with reverence. Mustangs and cattle, a place that was alive and successful.

"This guy's all mouth, boss. Don't worry. He can say whatever he wants, let him try and back it up." Reese picked up her wine and took a sip.

"Exactly," Dana agreed. "Anyone can see you're good fathers. Seriously. Those boys are happy and well-loved."

Connor took his hand and squeezed it, giving him a smile. "See? Don't worry, boss."

"Right? Lord. I'm trying. That plumb hurt my feelings."

Reese gasped. "You have feelings?"

"Hell, no. Cowboys don't have feelings," Connor teased.

"Or cowgirls." Dana snorted.

Early rolled his eyes, but it did feel so good, to have...a

building friendship, the idea that someone wanted this place to thrive too.

Connor kissed his fingers, let his hand go and refilled Dana's wine. "So when are you two moving in?"

"Demming is finishing his move out by Friday. Early said we can come in on Saturday. We don't have a ton of furniture yet, and Dana wants to paint some."

Demming was putting everything in a Pod and sending it west, then moving in with Early's parents. "Perfect. Have you and Demming figured out how much crossover there will be? I don't think he's given us a solid retirement date yet."

"He says he can give me two weeks, give or take. He wants to head out in time to help his daughter with things." Reese shrugged. "Whatever that means."

"Huh." Connor glanced at him. "What do you suppose that's about? Has he told you anything?"

Early shook his head, but he thought he might. He was afraid that Demming's daughter Emma, who he'd met dozens of times over the years, was in the middle of a divorce. He wasn't sure, though, so he wasn't going to spread rumors.

"Well, I hope she's okay. Are you all ready for one of Early's Mom's turnovers?" Connor was such a good host. The steaks had been great, the company was good, and Connor made sure that everyone had wine and conversation.

It was so nice to not have to think too hard, if Early was honest. This was so much easier than trying to deal with it on his own.

"Bring it on," Dana said with a laugh. "I've got a sweet tooth."

Reese snorted. "She's got more than one."

"I so do."

"I think you might have an admirer as well," Early muttered.

Dana blushed a bright pink, chin ducking. "It happens. I'm very careful not to tease or to encourage, but I hope that, in the future, they think of me in a kind way."

"They will. Jayden's just very aware of...pretty people lately." Connor grinned as he got up to go get dessert.

"If you only knew how many kids I've had to watch work through a crush on my wife..." Reese took Dana's hand.

"I'm the first new person a lot of them spend any real time with. It's special."

"It's adorable. I just didn't expect to have so much five-year-old competition."

Early laughed with Connor, even as Dana and Reese grinned at them.

They laid into Momma's goodies, and the conversation slowed for a while, all of them focused on the sweet pastries.

"This is nice. Early and I were—are—so upset about this shit with Ian. But you're good company. It's hard to focus on it."

Reese sighed softly, shook her head. "It sucks, having an asshole wandering around. At least we know what he looks like right? So we can keep him off the property."

"That's important. I don't want him anywhere near the kids." Connor shook his head.

"Of course not." That was, surprisingly, Dana. "No predators around the children. Not under any circumstances."

"So we know what we need to do here. Thanks, Dana. We appreciate the support. Sorry to drag you into this nonsense."

Reese waved one hand. "I have reason to want him beaten down, no worries."

"Turnovers?" Jayden hauled himself out of the pool. "Come on, Jax!"

"Uh-oh, here come the real troublemakers."

Early snorted as Jayden went, "Da-aa-ad!"

"Take one each and go sit at the little table, guys. And when you're done, it's shower time."

"What about the puppies? Should we take them out?"

Early rolled his eyes. "Tonight, yes. The dog run will be done tomorrow."

"Oh. Puppies. Did you see my Sophie?" Connor's eyes lit up.

"I did." Dana beamed at Connor. "I'll go pick up Molly this weekend. She's so sweet."

"We'll have a whole pack running around." Connor looked at him. "Demming will really have that run done by tomorrow? I don't know if I can put Sophie in it; those Labs might mistake her for a chew toy."

"His boys will, yeah. They've been together, babe. They'll be okay. I bet Sophie is fierce." Early thought that Connor was going to spoil that little girl to death.

"I guess we'll see." Connor shrugged.

Reese put her empty wine glass down. "We'd better get going. This has been a lot of fun."

"It has. Y'all be careful going back to your place."

"We will."

Dana stood and looked toward the kitchen. "Can we help with the dishes?"

Connor stood too. "Thank you, but no. We're good. I might be the only person on the planet that doesn't mind dishes. Thanks for bringing the cheese. Anyone who shows up with cheese is a friend of mine."

"Noted. I like to be friendly with my neighbors." Dana gave Connor a hug, then came to him. "Do I have to call you 'boss'?"

"Nope. Just Early."

Connor and Reese did the hug-or-handshake dance, and settled on some awkward combination of both, each of them laughing. "Let us know when you need some help with the move. We're here."

The devil that lived on Early's shoulder made him say, "We'll make Jayden lug boxes."

"Da-aa-dy! Ugh." Jayden groaned at him.

"Really, honey?" Connor rolled his eyes. "Go on and walk your pups, guys."

"Okay, Daddy. Goldie! Brownie! Let's go poop!" Jaxson sounded joyous.

They walked Reese and Dana out to their truck. "Drive safe. We'll see you soon." Connor put an arm around his waist as they watched the truck head down the drive. "That was nice."

"It was. I think they'll be a good addition to the family."

"They will. Maybe we should just hire Dana to teach school on the ranch for the rest of our additions." Connor tickled him and ran for the front porch.

"Oh ho!" He gave chase, loving the way Connor's laugh followed him.

Connor stopped on the top step and turned around. "Damn. You've gotten faster since you moved out here."

"I have to be able to avoid bulls, you know?"

"It's hot. You're a stud of a cowboy, you know that?" How did Connor do that—turn a playful moment into something so sexy?

"I'm yours, so I'll take it." He didn't care if anyone else, ever, thought he was blistering.

"You are. And I know that." Connor pulled him closer. "I know, okay? Zero doubt. Ever. So don't stress it."

He held on. "I just—I never ever want you to doubt us. We're important."

That faith was the bedrock they stood on together.

"I couldn't. Not for a minute. We're body and soul, you and I. We'll protect what's ours." Connor squeezed him hard.

"Ew are you going to kiss again? Can you wait until I'm in bed, please?" Jayden opened the door, and the puppies ran into the house.

"More and more kisses. Kisses and smoochies and snoggeroonis." Early loved teasing them.

Jayden rolled his eyes and handed Connor Sophie's leash. "She's cute, Dad, but she's tiny."

"She is, right?" Connor smiled and picked her up. "Who's the cutest? Showers, boys, and bed. We'll come tuck you in."

"Okay!" Jaxson ran in, but Jayden lingered.

"Hey, Daddy? Dad? Thank you. They're so amazing."

Connor pointed to him. "This was all Daddy. He's been looking for puppies for you for a while."

"It's—you're the best." Jayden ran to him, hugging him hard. "I love it here. I love my life."

Connor smiled at him. "It's a pretty good life."

"It's the best." And Early intended to keep it.

24

Connor sat on the front porch, watching Sophie sniff around. She couldn't get very far from him on her leash, but she was tiny, so she didn't need a lot of lead to stretch her legs.

He was supposed to be working. He had his laptop open to a half-finished fancy budgeting spreadsheet he was putting together for his first meeting with Reese tomorrow. Instead, he was watching Sophie and admiring the view of the mustangs and the mountains in the background.

Early was out on the land, running some tests on the water, and the kids were in school. The Labs were in the dog run, and it was just gorgeous out here in the sun. It was the first real quiet he'd had in a while, and he was enjoying it.

His quiet was interrupted though, by a truck coming up the drive. A visitor ought to drive right up to the house, but the truck stopped about halfway, close enough that he could see it well but not the driver.

Were they lost? Did they make a wrong turn? He stood up and waved, figuring he'd let whoever it was know he was there.

Whoever it was coming seemed to be waving a piece of paper and a something else. Weird. They needed a camera out there, so he could just see on his phone.

He moved to the edge of the porch and slowly, made sure Sophie was secure, then made his way down the steps. There was something strange going on and he wasn't going to move too far from the house. He pulled out his phone and texted Early.

> Blue pickup in the driveway. Older model...
> know it?

> Shoot me a pic

He did, and just before the man got close enough, Connor got the text.

> Ian. OMW

Ian? What the actual fuck was he doing here? Connor stood his ground, eyes narrowing as he got a good look at the driver. He had nothing to say, so he said nothing, waiting to see what the asshole was up to.

"Where the fuck is that bastard? I will not be disrespected like this! We were lovers!"

He raised an eyebrow and started to laugh. "Get off my property."

"Don't you laugh at me!"

What? Was this guy going to announce he was pregnant with Early's baby?

Now that he was getting a look at the guy that rage he'd felt the other day was replaced with something else. Ian was ridiculous. "Get back in your piece of shit truck and get off my property. You're trespassing."

"I'm going to make you sorry you ever came here!" Ian stood at the fence near the house with a pair of wire cutters, and he started cutting the wires of their fence.

Oh, that was perfect. He snapped a picture, then called the sheriff.

Ian was making this way too easy.

Connor gave Early a wave as he rode up, flying up the pasture on a sleek black beast. He pointed to where Ian was slowly destroying their fence, and then to his phone. Early flung himself off the horse like a bulldogger, heading straight for Ian.

That was the hottest fucking thing he'd ever seen his husband do.

He talked calmly with the sheriff's office who said they'd send someone up right away. "I would hurry. Early's not looking too forgiving."

Ian was talking hard, but Early was having none of it, and the low snarl as Early swatted the wire cutters away from the fence.

Damn. This was going to be jerk-off material for the next ten years.

He took a few steps closer, ostensibly so he could hear what they were saying, but really it was to get a whiff of those pheromones. "Hey, honey. We'll have some company in a minute."

"Good deal. You touch me with those wire cutters, you little fuck, and I will bury you in the ground."

"You should have let me stay. You liked me. The kids liked me. This is all his fault!" Ian thrust the cutters in his direction, but he was nowhere near close enough that Ian could hurt him.

He wanted to snarl at Ian about the kids, but he didn't, he kept his cool and let Early do the snarling.

"You're a stupid shit, and you're threatening my happy ass with a weapon." Early wasn't yelling. In fact, there was a solid, deep calm in his lover's voice.

"Shut up," Ian shouted.

"I think he's pouting." Connor snorted. "Don't you have any friends, Ian? Someone should have talked you out of this." There were two cars coming up the drive, one of them had flashing lights.

"You called the cops?"

"Dude, clean out your ears. Who did you think Connor meant by company?"

Ian tried to run for his truck, but Connor stepped right in his way, stopping him short. "Nope."

The wire cutters flashed as Ian raised them, and Early stepped in, stopping the arc of the weapon on the way down, and then Early coldcocked him, flattening him out with a single blow. "I don't think so, asshole."

Connor's cock had a strong opinion about that move, but the cops were pulling up, so he did his best to ignore it. He stared at Ian lying there for a second, then burst into wild laughter. "Oh my fucking god. I was worried about that guy?"

"Goddamn, Early!" The deputy, who was a young man with huge brown eyes. "This is that guy you were telling me about?"

"It is. I want to press charges. He cut my fence, he threatened my husband, and he cut me."

Early raised his arm, and sure enough, there was a long scratch that was *just* deep enough to bleed.

"And he's trespassing, so we want to file for a restraining order too."

The deputy knelt next to Ian and checked his pulse, then patted Ian's face a couple of times, and when Ian groaned, the deputy rolled him over. "He's okay. Let me get him in the car before he causes any more trouble." Then Early got a wicked grin. "You need the hospital, bud?"

"Kiss my skinny butt, Delroy."

Delroy rolled his eyes. "Nah, that's Mr. Pretty's job."

He rolled his eyes, but he had to laugh. Early knew literally everyone. "Yeah, I'll take good care of him."

Delroy hauled Ian to his feet. "Is that his truck? I'll send a rig."

"Don't touch my truck."

"You're under arrest, buddy."

"What? I live here..." Delroy shook his head and dragged Ian off to the squad car with the flashing lights. "He hit me!"

"We saw the fight, man. You started it. He's pressing charges."

Early snorted, then went to the horse that was just eating grass. "Hey, sweetheart. You okay?"

The beast lifted his head, lipped Early's shoulder, then nudged him hard.

"I know. You ran fast, didn't you?"

Connor sauntered over and out an arm around Early's waist, then leaned up and whispered. "You're a fucking stud, husband, and when this nonsense is over and the cops are gone, I want you to take me to bed." The kids wouldn't be home for hours.

"Oh, naughty, naughty. You liked that, did you?" Early's cheeks heated, and he leaned into Connor.

He chuckled. "I've seen you ride," he said, his words intentional. "But never like that."

"Mmm... I like this. I'll have to take her over to Reese. Let someone brush her out."

He nodded. "I can finish up here. I'll wait for you on the porch. Don't dawdle, this is a bit...urgent." He'd handle the deputy. The restraining order he'd have to go to the station for tomorrow anyway.

"I'll be up in the bedroom and naked before you notice I'm gone."

Connor laughed loud enough he got the deputy's attention.

"You have a minute?"

"I do. A minute...that asshole doesn't deserve much more of my time." He gave Early's ass a pat and made his way to the squad car.

They'd take care of this shit, then he was taking Early upstairs to ride.

25

"Daddy! We're going over to that truck! They have full-sized Hershey's bars!"

Just what Jaxson, aka the littlest Hulk, needed. More sugar.

"I'm coming, son." He didn't have to dress up, but he did have to follow along behind his two Avengers, just to make sure.

"They got Twix?"

Who knew Captain America had such a sweet tooth?

"I'm glad we sprung for the decent dental insurance."

He grinned back at his husband. "I hear you. Just think about how much another hooligan's mouth is going to cost us."

"Another hooligan or *two*." Connor grinned right back at him.

"So, when are you two building the enclosure for your pool so my kids can still spend the night and swim?" Mike sauntered over as two more Avengers ran after Jayden and Jaxson. Between them they almost had the whole assembly.

"They can spend the night and watch movies. We're busy planning how to build our family."

"You really are gluttons for punishment, huh?" Mike laughed.

Connor shrugged. "You mean Lauren isn't asking you for more after the twins and your new one?"

Mike shook his head. "We have our hands full I think."

The boys moved as a group from one truck to the next. The last one in line was a big fire truck all decked out to look like a haunted mansion.

"So you say... I thought we were done too, and then we moved out here."

Mike snorted. "Damn, Connor. It's almost like you like being on the PTO."

Early snorted. "He just saw that new baby of yours and melted."

Not that Early blamed him at all. That little one was about pretty.

"Well, we never had baby-babies, you know? We got the boys young, but they were kids." Connor got that distracted look—the one Early thought of as his baby fever look—and smiled. "I'd like a couple of wee Earlys too."

"That would be amazing. I wish you two the best of luck."

Early's cheeks just burned, but honestly, him too. He would love more babies. "Thanks, man. You'll be the third to know—after the boys and the grandparents."

"And Reese and Dana."

"Right." Those two were already family, and Early loved how they fit right in. "After boys, grandparents, and Reese and the wife."

Early glanced at Connor, and suddenly he couldn't hardly breathe.

He was home. Finally. Blessedly. And they all were together and happy.

"Daddy! Dad! Come *on!*"

"Coming, boys. Connor, love! Come *on!*"

There was a lifetime of goodies to be had.

WANT MORE BA & JODI?

Interested in learning more about our East Meets Westerns?

Join BA & Jodi's Newsletter
https://lp.constantcontactpages.com/sl/nzvRTTy

Patreon: https://www.patreon.com/BATortuga
There are lots of tiers to chose from, and also free serial stories.
Discord: https://discord.gg/Vba5P5Qv
BA's Discord server has a channel for BA/Jodi related chat and info.

Hey, Y'all!

We want to thank you for giving Home Free a try. We hope you enjoyed the story and want to check out the rest of the series.

If you can spare a few minutes to post a review at the retail website where you made your purchase, we'd very much appreciate it!

Yeehaw and thanks for reading!

BA & Jodi

ABOUT JODI

JODI takes herself way too seriously and has been known to randomly break out in song. Her queer MCs are imperfect but genuine, stubborn but likable, often kinky, and frequently their own worst enemies. They are characters you can't help but fall in love with while they stumble along the path to their happily ever after. For those looking to get on her good side, Jodi's obsessions include nonfat lattes, basketball (go Celtics!), and tequila any way you pour it.

Website: jodipayne.net
Newsletter: https://readerlinks.com/l/2317334
All Jodi's Social Links: linktr.ee/jodipayne

ABOUT BA

Western to the bone and an unrepentant Daddy's Girl, BA Tortuga spends her days with her hounds and her beloved wife, having mother-daughter dates, and eating Mexican food. When she's not doing that, she's writing. She spends her days off watching rodeo, knitting, and surfing Pinterest in the name of research. Following their own personal joys, BA and Julia heard the call of the high desert and they now live in the New Mexico mountains. BA's personal saviors include her wife, her best friends, and coffee. Lots of coffee. Really good coffee.

Having written everything from fist-fighting cowboys to rural single dads to werewolves, BA does her damnedest to tell the stories of her heart, which is committed to giving everyone their happily ever after. With books ranging from heart-warming stories of found families, to rodeo cowboys that are fighting to make a mark, to fiery passionate love affairs, BA refuses to be pigeon-holed by anyone but the voices in her head.

BA loves to talk to her readers and can be found at http://batortuga.com/ and her newsletter signup link is http://bit.ly/BAJulianews

AVAILABLE FROM JODI & BA

East Meets Westerns

The On the Ranch Series

Tending Tyler

Roped In

Diamonds in the Rough

Outfoxed

The Wrecked Universe

Wrecked

Flying Blind

Special Delivery, A Wrecked Holiday Novel

Seeds and Sunshine

Pickup Man

Cowboy for Sale

The Merry Everything Series

Window Dressing

Cowboy Protection

Cowboys and Cupcakes

Thawed Out

A Present for Parker - Coming January 2026!

The Higher Elevation Series

Heart of a Cowboy

Keeping Promises

Bigger Than Us

Home Free

BDSM/Kink

The Cowboy and the Dom Trilogy

First Rodeo, Book One

Razor's Edge, Book Two

No Ghosts, Book Three

The Soldier and the Angel, a Cowboy and Dom Novel

The Sin Deep Series

(set in The Cowboy and the Dom Universe)

Sin Deep

Trouble with Cowboys

The Triskelion Series

Breaking the Rules

Making a Mark

Making the Rules

Les's Bar Series

Just Dex

Hide Bound

Wholly Trinity

New Tricks

Lost Boy

The Barn Series

Zeke & Wesley

Other Titles

The Collaborations Series

Refraction

Syncopation

Puzzles Series

Cryptic

Single Titles

Temptation Ranch

Land of Enchantment

Summit Springs Sapphic (F/F) Romance

Christmas Bizarre

Honeymoon in the Cards